mys

"He's fine—we're going out tomorrow night."

He glared at her through narrowed eyes. "That's great," he snapped.

Kate almost blurted out the truth, then put a hand up to cover her mouth. Following him out to his car, she told herself not to be silly. She had to concentrate on her plan. Finding Mr. Right might take some time, but it wasn't impossible.

In the meantime, all she had to do was steer clear of Mr. Wrong—and that meant Brady.

Dear Reader,

At Silhouette Romance we're celebrating the start of 1994 with a wonderful lineup of exciting love stories. Get set for a year filled with terrific books by the authors you love best, and brand-new names you'll be delighted to discover.

Those FABULOUS FATHERS continue, with Linc Rider in Kristin Morgan's *Rebel Dad*. Linc was a mysterious drifter who entered the lives of widowed Jillian Fontenot and her adopted son. Little did Jillian know he was a father in search of a child—*her* child.

Pepper Adams is back with *Lady Willpower*. In this charming battle of wills, Mayor Joe Morgan meets his match when Rachel Fox comes to his town and changes it—and Joe!

It's a story of love lost and found in Marie Ferrarella's *Aunt Connie's Wedding*. Carole Anne Wellsley was home for her aunt's wedding, and Dr. Jefferson Drumm wasn't letting her get away again!

And don't miss Rebecca Daniels's *Loving the Enemy*. This popular Intimate Moments author brings her special brand of passion to the Silhouette Romance line. Rounding out the month, look for books by Geeta Kingsley and Jude Randal.

We hope that you'll be joining us in the coming months for books by Diana Palmer, Elizabeth August, Suzanne Carey and many more of your favorite authors.

Anne Canadeo
Senior Editor

Please address questions and book requests to:
Reader Service
U.S.: P.O. Box 1325, Buffalo, NY 14269
Canadian: P.O. Box 1050, Niagara Falls, Ont. L2E 7G7

MR. WRONG
Geeta Kingsley

Silhouette
ROMANCE™
Published by Silhouette Books
America's Publisher of Contemporary Romance

In memory of my nephew, Sukhi, who will live
forever in the hearts of those who love him

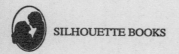 SILHOUETTE BOOKS

ISBN 0-373-08985-6

MR. WRONG

Copyright © 1994 by Geeta M. Kakade

Printed in U.S.A.

GEETA KINGSLEY

is a former elementary school teacher who loves traveling, music, needlework and gardening. Raised in an army family, she was never lonely as long as she had books to read. She now lives in Southern California with her husband, two teenagers and the family dog. Her first published novel, *Faith, Hope and Love,* was a finalist in the Romance Writers of America's RITA competition.

Geeta believes in the triumph of the human spirit, and this, along with her concern for the environment, is reflected in her characters and stories.

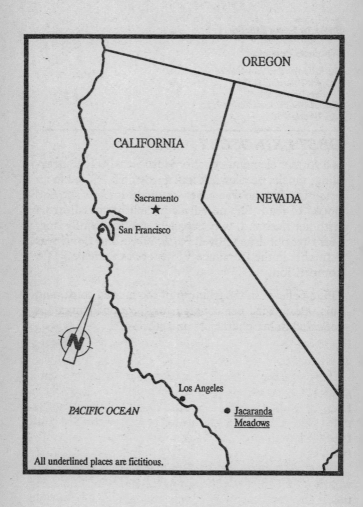

OREGON

CALIFORNIA

Sacramento
★

San Francisco

NEVADA

Los Angeles

PACIFIC OCEAN

Jacaranda
Meadows

All underlined places are fictitious.

Chapter One

Watching the store for his mother wasn't Brady's choice. He had so many better ways of spending a Sunday afternoon, but Mom could talk anyone, including him, into anything. The trait ran in the family...it had to do with being part Irish. Her assistant manager was sick, another salesperson was on vacation and Mom was giving a party that evening. Besides, she'd pointed out, Brady could relax just as easily at the store. January was a slow time of year.

Checking the back door of Bernie's Gifts and Luggage, Brady switched off the lights before heading for the front. It hadn't been as bad as his legal mind had anticipated, though. Mom had covered every eventuality from fire, to how to close the back window, which had a difficult bolt.

What she hadn't covered, Brady realized suddenly, was what to do if there was a foot in the doorway at closing time. The foot in question was encased in a light blue canvas shoe. Throwing open the door he'd been about to shut, Brady's gaze traced a path up slim ankles, long lovely legs, heart-stopping knees and slender thighs. He couldn't remember ever thinking of knees as sexy, but these were. Beautifully, gloriously sexy.

Reluctantly his eyes continued their journey north. The satisfyingly miniscule blue shorts she wore were the kind that ought to be given away free to those who qualified for it. The elastic waistband defined a waist that he could span with his hands. Perky breasts lifted the faded, blue-and-white checked shirt tucked into the shorts.

Red hair hung in a silky curtain to the edge of her shorts. As forest-green eyes met his, he heard a distinct cymbal clash of emotion in the far reaches of his brain. Brady's breath left his body in a small surprised whoosh.

"Are you open?" Worry didn't disguise the husky softness of her voice. "The sign in your window says Sundays: 12-5. It's still one minute to five. I fell asleep, otherwise I would have been here much earlier."

"Of course we're open." Brady stood aside. Could she hear him above the drumroll of his heart?

She smiled at him uncertainly, revealing deep dimples placed unusually high on the inverted crescent of her cheeks. The tiny gap between her two front teeth enchanted him. Brady's hands clenched at the totally unexpected assault on his senses.

"Thank you." She entered the store, and his nostrils filled with the scent of lilacs. He recognized it, because his mother had always had lilac bushes planted in the yard of every house they'd lived in.

Brady switched the lights back on and glanced down at his wrist as he followed her back into the store. The hands of his expensive Swiss watch, always precise, showed it was exactly three minutes *past* five. She came to a halt in front of one of the showcases.

"I have to pick up a present for my fiancé."

His gaze narrowed as she wet her lips and said quickly, "Well, almost-fiancé. It's Harold's birthday tonight, and a great deal depends on everything being perfect."

The term "almost-fiancé" intrigued Brady. Not only because it was a phrase he'd never heard before, but because there was a great deal of opportunity between "almost" and "fiancé." A great deal. And Brady Gallagher wasn't a man to ignore his opportunities.

"This won't take a minute," she said quickly. "I know exactly what I want."

One of Brady's eyebrows went up as she pointed to a writing case in a glass cabinet. "That's the one."

Leather. Expensive. Ostentatious.

It wasn't the kind of thing he would have imagined her choosing.

Kate watched the salesman go through the bunch of keys, trying to find the right one that would unlock the display case.

It gave her a respite from those intense charcoal-rimmed gray eyes that seemed to see all the way into her brain and heart. *Intense* was putting it mildly.

Kate thought she heard him swear softly as he tried yet another key. She bit her lip to stop herself from smiling. He must be new.

"Nice," had been her first thought when she'd seen him. Something flexed in the pit of her stomach in protest. Kate amended that to *very* nice.

He really needn't have let her in. His looks had jogged her senses, but it was his niceness that wrapped her heart in a swathe of crushed velvet now. Maybe that was why she could talk to him so freely.

He was taller than her by a head, well built without being overly muscular. His black hair was thick and wavy. Made to run one's hands through. A knock-'em-dead smile and those intense eyes completed the picture of overpowering charm and power.

He looked up, his gaze laser-beaming its way to her soul. The responsive surge of feeling in her body confounded Kate. She wanted to know this man better. *Yes,* thumped her wayward heart. *Yes, please!*

No, warned her brain. *No! He's Mr. Wrong.*

Kate turned away, rubbing the back of her neck, where tension gathered with hurricanelike strength.

He had to be new here. She would have remembered if she had seen him before. He didn't look like your normal kind of salesman, either, but then one could never tell these days.

Trying to distract herself, Kate took her mind back over the afternoon. Lying down for a few minutes had been a terrible mistake. Cleaning her apartment, on top of a fast-paced three-mile walk, had worn her out. Bolting awake at four-forty-five, she'd remembered Harold's present and had catapulted out of the apartment. To go without one would be unthinkable.

Kate had broken the speed limit to get here before the store closed. As she'd parked her old Ford and run to the store, she'd seen the lights being switched off. Her foot in the doorway had been a last-ditch attempt to get in. Luckily it had worked.

The man's survey had made Kate very conscious of the old shorts she had donned that morning. They were perfect garb for cleaning her apartment, but not suitable to go shopping in. When she'd originally bought them, she'd been eighteen and there had been more of the shorts and less of her. Kate realized there was nothing she could do about that now. She hadn't even had time to think of changing.

"Thank you," she said, as he finally put the writing case she'd pointed out into her hands.

Brady watched her turn it over to check it. Her look of dismay as she checked the price tag didn't escape him.

"We have some really nice men's wallets," he offered.

She looked up and flushed. "Oh, this is fine...really."

Out of habit, Brady put two and two together. The only reason she'd be so particular about getting the case would be if she wanted to impress Harold. Which meant she wasn't as sure of the "almost" part as she sounded.

It was time to find out more.

"What did you say Harold's last name was?"

She hadn't and they both knew it, but she supplied it now. "Benson."

Brady frowned. "Does he have an office here? The name sounds really familiar."

She fell into the trap. "Harold's a real-estate broker. He has one office here and another in Orange."

A little thing like reluctance on her part to answer his questions didn't deter Brady. He had to find out more about this Harold. "Known him long?" What he *really* wanted to know was, had she fallen in love immediately? He saw her eyes widen at his tone.

"When you said you were getting engaged, I just assumed you knew Harold really well. I mean, one can't be too sure these days, can one?" Inwardly, he winced. At thirty, he had no right to sound like an uncle.

"Harold's well-known in the area."

She still hadn't mentioned love.

"And rich, too, I'll bet."

He said the words, making a little test out of them. Money was definitely a criterion for all the women he knew. It turned them on quicker than a man could run from them.

A frown pleated her brow, accompanying the flash of temper in her eyes. "What's wrong with being rich?"

The question reminded him he had better concentrate on minding his own business, no matter how tempting the woman in front of him might be. "Nothing."

"It's important to have ambition and drive."

His good intentions lasted all of five seconds.

"And this gift is going to show him how much you care?" Brady couldn't prevent the edge of sarcasm in his voice. A part of him was aware he was treating her as if she were a witness in the stand, and yet he couldn't stop.

She looked at him and he saw the deadly seriousness in her eyes as she nodded.

It was like having an icy-cold shower after being in a warm spa. He hadn't misjudged anyone so badly since his first case when he'd represented a crook, believing everything the man had told him. The lamb in front of him was really a disguised she-wolf. The thought took the lid off Brady's temper.

"Is the gift some sort of investment in your future?"

"Investment?" she echoed blankly.

"Yes," said Brady impatiently. "Is getting this writing case going to convince Harold how much you care?"

She caught her lower lip with her teeth, let it go. The tiny action heated Brady's blood.

"Things like this are important," she said quietly. "Maybe Harold will propose tonight."

Maybe? When two people were in love there was no maybe about it. Which reminded him, she still hadn't mentioned the word.

"Are you in love with Harold?" he asked angrily. He didn't care that it wasn't any of his business, that he didn't even know who she was. He had to know. Hearing her say the words was the only thing that would kill this last lingering spark of attraction inside him.

"Not yet, but I will be," she said coolly.

The simple admission rocked him. He may as well hear more about her extraordinary blueprint for life and love. "Oh? Is that stage two of your plan?"

"Yes." Kate couldn't understand why he was so angry. She looked at him, assessing him silently. He had barged into a personal area of her life and was examining it as if he had every right to do so.

Something inside Brady froze as he looked at her. In his circle he'd met many women who looked for advantageous relationships. He'd never met one who admitted it as coolly as this green-eyed mermaid did, though. How could he have thought her soft? She was living proof that there were very few women like his mother and sister left. Women who believed love was the main reason—the only *real* reason—to marry someone.

This woman was looking for a meal ticket for the rest of her life. A *gourmet* meal ticket. His anger erupted into a blaze.

She read his expression correctly because her voice turned defensive. "Financial stability is very important in a happy marriage."

"Does love have any place on this blueprint of yours?" Brady demanded.

"Given the right climate, love grows," she assured him, taking out her checkbook.

His expression conveyed he wanted to shake her. The charcoal-rimmed eyes dropped to her mouth, their message unmistakable. When he looked at her again, Kate recognized the desire mixed with anger in his eyes. A pulse erupted at the base of her neck. She felt herself flush from head to toe. It was time to take control of the situation.

"How much do I owe you?"

He rang up the sale on the cash register and read her name upside down as she made out the check. Kathryn Langdon.

As she handed the check over, Brady heard a sound at the front of the store and glanced up.

Henrietta Cooper, owner of the hairstyling salon next door, called out from the door. "Are you having a problem closing up, Brady?"

"No problem," Brady said quickly. "I'm just attending to one last customer."

"Kate Langdon, is that you?"

Henrietta came into the store. Brady sighed. The woman was a walking information exchange. With her around, Jacaranda Meadows didn't need a local newspaper.

"It's a shame you won't be working at the preschool anymore, Kate. My grandson Billy's going to miss you something awful. He told me how you made the other kids stop teasing him about his lisp."

So, Kate Langdon was a preschool teacher? Brady's interest surged again, though he did his best to hide it.

"Have you heard from Bettie May Walter recently?"

"No."

"Her dad was in for a haircut yesterday. Told me how much time you spent with her. It seems you talked to her about those kids she was hanging out with. Bettie May said you insisted she talk to her counselor at school. Tom's that relieved she took your advice. He hasn't been able to do a thing with her since his wife left. Things are better now."

"I'm glad."

She sounded embarrassed, not happy. Brady frowned. Henrietta's words made Kate Langdon sound like a giver, not a taker. What was going on?

"This recession has too many people unemployed," Henrietta Cooper continued. "They can't afford pre-school for their kids when they're out of work. Too bad it means you won't be able to work there, though. Alma Hunt told me she had to let you go, because you're the newest teacher." Henrietta eyed the package in Kate's hands. "Do you still baby-sit on the weekends?"

"Yes."

Henrietta nodded. "That was a clever idea you came up with. Mrs. Harrison, the doctor's wife, can't stop praising you. It's a boon for busy parents to have a responsible adult to leave their children with, and get away for a weekend now and then."

Kate muttered something, and Henrietta went on. "Luckily for you, you have that nice apartment rent-free, in exchange for house-sitting for that traveling couple. What's their name again?"

"Guthrie. Samantha and Pete Guthrie."

The conversation immersed Brady in further confusion. Henrietta painted a completely different picture of Kate than the one talking with her had given him. There was also the first impression he'd received. Which, of the three, was the real Kate? The innocent but sultry late shopper, the cold and calculating husband-seeker or the warm-hearted teacher? It might be worth finding out. He was, after all, in Jacaranda Meadows for a while and everyone was innocent till proven guilty.

"Are you pretty much booked up with the baby-sitting?" he heard Henrietta ask.

"Things are slow now."

"That's a shame. What'll you do?"

The look on Kate Langdon's face indicated to Brady that she needed rescuing from Henrietta's compulsion to know everything about everyone. He decided he'd save her.

"Do you need anything more? Wrapping paper, ribbon?" he interjected, as Henrietta opened her mouth again.

There was gratitude in Kate's glance as she said, "I have everything else. Thank you for letting me in."

Henrietta turned to leave with Kate. Brady stiffened. Once outside, he could depend on Henrietta to mention he was a lawyer, and that his mother owned Bernie's. Brady didn't want Kate Langdon being filled in on his background just yet.

The check in his hand gave him an idea. "I'll need two IDs," he said quickly.

"Of course." Kate put her package down, and took out her credit-card holder.

"I'll leave you to it. Harry's getting impatient." Henrietta turned away reluctantly as they heard a car horn toot outside for the third time.

"I'm coming, I'm coming," Henrietta grumbled as she walked out. "Why'd I have to go and marry one of those silent types who doesn't understand the joys of conversation? He's always tootin' that stupid horn. You'd think he'd been born with his hand glued to it."

Kate and Brady couldn't help smiling over Henrietta's remarks. Kate felt the color come up under her skin as her gaze tangled with Brady's. His smile was knockout quality. For one crazy moment, she wondered what it would be like to have that mobile mouth pressed against hers.

Shocked by her own thoughts, Kate looked down. She had to find something other than this disturbing man to focus on. Her gaze fell on the glass paperweights near the cash register. Inside them were tiny pressed blue and purple wildflowers, their delicacy a direct contrast to the thick glass they were encased in. Running a finger over the smooth surface of one of them, Kate wondered how the flowers had been imprisoned in the glass without being destroyed.

Now this, she thought, *this is what I would have liked to have given Harold.* Picking it up, she turned it over and noticed the price. Under five dollars. It would never do.

Looking up, she saw Brady watching her. Had he guessed the drift of her thoughts? Kate felt some unknown emotion weave a tenuous web around them, as fragile as the flowers in the glass paperweight. Confusion shivered through her and she thought, with those eyes he'll never need words to make love with. Those eyes say it all.

Guilt flooded Kate. Now where on earth had that thought come from, for heaven's sake? Harold was her future; this man, Brady, only an extra fluffy cloud on the day's horizon. The way she felt around him, hot one minute, cold the next, was irrational. The nap had definitely addled her brain. She'd better get a grip on herself. Her plans were already made and no one was going to change them.

"Thank you for letting me in."

Words were better than this silence that seemed to breed tantalizing, impossible pictures, coloring them with the breath of danger.

"It's no problem." The words dismissed what he'd done, and he hurried on to his next question, "Where do you teach preschool?"

"In Jacaranda Meadows," she said. "I'm taking classes at the local college. I'm going to be a fully fledged teacher one day."

Brady frowned at the quiet pride in her voice. He had another piece that didn't fit. If money was so important, why not a more lucrative career?

"Why a teacher?"

"I like being around children." A quick look at her watch and she picked up her driver's license and the credit card she'd handed Brady earlier. "I have to run. Harold's picking me up at six sharp and he hates to be kept waiting. Thank you again, and goodbye. You've been very kind."

"Not goodbye," Brady said softly to her retreating back. "It's hello."

His Irish instincts told him he was going to see more of Kate Langdon. He had to.

As Brady memorized the address on Kate's check, he heard a sound and looked up.

"I didn't close my door properly and now my car won't start." Panic showed on Kate's face as she came back into the store. The glance she threw at the clock on the wall was desperate. "May I use your telephone to call a tow truck?"

"Why don't I look at it?" Brady suggested. "If the battery's down, all it needs is a jump start. I've got a pair of jumper cables in my car."

He felt embarrassed by the sudden moisture that flooded her eyes. Lifting one hand, she tucked a strand of hair behind one ear. "You're very kind."

"And devious as a leprechaun," Brady muttered to himself as he turned off the lights, locked the store and followed Kate out to her car.

He was familiar with the routine in the fairy tales he read his four-year-old nephew. Man rescues woman in distress. Woman falls in love with rescuer. They live happily ever after.

Brady lifted the hood of her car and said, "Let me get my car. I'll be right back."

Driving his BMW over from the tree he had parked it under, Brady aligned it next to the old Ford. As he took the jumper cables from the trunk and straightened them, he heard Kate Langdon say, "Nice car."

"I borrowed it from a friend," Brady blurted out. No sense in ruining his cover yet. He wanted to keep up the pretense of being a salesman.

Kate watched Brady as he bent over her car. Why was he going out of his way to be helpful? She couldn't remember a time when someone had actually looked out for her. Strength, plus kindness, were formidable forces in a man.

For the second time that day, Kate felt guilt flood her. She was attaching too much importance to a man she would probably never see again. Harold was the one for her. She had to remember that!

She waited till Brady had the cables in position, and then switched his car on before she started hers. To her relief, the old engine soon roared to life.

Removing the jumper cables, Brady said, "You're all set. Have fun."

Kate swallowed. "Thank you."

Getting into her car, Kate backed out of the space she'd parked in. Brady, when she looked at him, raised one hand and waved to her. Kate felt herself go hot. The man's charm was deadly.

* * *

Thirty minutes later, Kate stood in front of the mirror, wishing she was one of those tiny women who brought out a man's protective side. At five-nine, she didn't have a spare ounce of fat on her, but next to Harold's mother, rake thin and impossibly beautiful, she felt like a giant.

Kate tugged at the neck of the peacock-blue silk top she wore with a black velvet skirt. Nervousness was building up inside like a storm in the offing.

The meeting with Brady was responsible for this turmoil inside her. He'd made her self-conscious about her intentions, but she had to put the earlier conversation out of her mind. She would be fine as soon as Harold arrived to pick her up. They were eating at his mother's house tonight, a fact that increased Kate's uneasiness.

Taking inventory of her features didn't help. Her eyes and her dimples were her best bets. Her nose and mouth were tolerable, but she hated the tiny gap between her two front teeth. She couldn't help that, because orthodontists charged exorbitant rates for braces. There wasn't much she could do with her straight red hair, either, except tie it back or braid it.

Smoothing the black skirt over hips that suddenly seemed too big, Kate sucked in her breath and turned for a sideways look at herself. Momentarily another picture flashed across her mental screen. Eyes the color of slate, filled with blatant appreciation, caressing where they rested, as their owner asked her if she needed anything else.

She hadn't been mistaken. In the beginning, Brady had liked her. Very much.

Kate tugged at the neckline of her top again. Being honest was very important. She wasn't sorry she had told him about her plans, though it had hurt to see Brady's eyes darken, his jaw clench in dislike. He obviously didn't approve of her blueprint for Mr. Right.

Kate bit her lip hard to make herself stop thinking about the man. He was a stranger. His opinion wasn't important. Her plans were. She wanted to marry someone who was financially secure so her children wouldn't grow up like she had. Poverty wasn't the best backdrop for mental well-being. The memory of the years of domestic violence she'd been exposed to added to that, and made Kate very sure of what she wanted.

Marriage to Harold would ensure a secure future.

A picture of Brady looking down at her as he stood by her car door, intruded suddenly. He had ignited a spark within her that refused to be put out. She had never thought one could feel so... so alive in the presence of a man.

"Have fun," he'd said, but his expression had been ambiguous, as if he hadn't really meant it. His eyes had said a great deal more, as they'd dropped to her mouth.

The doorbell provided welcome relief from her thoughts. Kate hurried to the door, telling herself she shouldn't have overdone the cleaning. Tiredness was the only explanation for the sudden urge to cry.

Chapter Two

Brady stretched his legs in his parents' whirlpool and took a sip of ice-cold beer. Mom was in the kitchen putting the finishing touches to the party that was to start in an hour's time. Dad was still out playing golf.

Brady didn't mind being alone. He was trying to think up some way of getting in touch with Kate Langdon again. ASAP.

Brady looked up as his sister, Maura, burst through the patio door. "Hi!" he said lazily.

"Brady, you'll never believe what's happened." Maura always spoke fast...as if she had to, or life would run away from her.

"No, I won't," Brady agreed, smiling into his sister's gray-green eyes.

"Jack's company is sending him to Australia and New Zealand and they're willing to pay for my ticket, as well. Only..."

"Only what?" Jack was vice president of marketing for a company that manufactured software, but Brady couldn't see where his sister was going with this.

"It's Cody. We're going to be constantly on the move in those six weeks and it's going to be too much for him. You know how he is when he's cooped up."

Brady could testify to that. He had volunteered to spend time with his nephew when Cody had had the chicken pox. The four-year-old had not been easy to entertain. Staying indoors and resting were bad words in Cody's book.

"Mom would offer to watch him like a shot," Maura said, "but she's got the shop. It isn't fair to expect her to take him along there. Even if she does, you know Cody. He can get too much for her and Dad."

"I remember the time you left him with them for a week. By the end of it, there were six varieties of ice cream in the freezer because Cody had said he liked them all."

Maura smiled. "Isn't it strange how the same people who were so strict with us, are like putty in their grandson's hands?"

Brady nodded. He knew Maura's reluctance to leave Cody with their parents wasn't based simply on the amount of spoiling he'd get. Maura, Brady and Jack all agreed the parents had put in their share of doing, and were entitled to a peaceful retirement. Unless it was an emergency, they were not to be bothered.

"Any ideas, big brother?"

As he looked at Maura's flushed face, Brady realized he had the perfect solution. Talk about luck!

"What if you hire someone to take care of him during the day? Mom and Dad can manage him from five in the evening till the next morning."

"Who can I get at such short notice?" Maura asked doubtfully. "You know the last two baby-sitters told us not to call them again. Cody doesn't like people who sit and watch television, and tell him to play with his toys and be a good boy. It brings out the worst in him."

Brady knew Cody's worst could be formidable . . . like tying a baby-sitter's shoelaces together, or filling her bag with whipped cream.

"I'm not thinking of a regular baby-sitter. I met a preschool teacher today who takes care of kids when their parents are away."

Maura's eyes narrowed. "How old is she?"

Katie was twenty-four. He'd seen her date of birth on her driver's license. "About your age. I think you'd like her. Why not meet her and decide?"

Brady saw the sliver of hope in Maura's eyes. "It might just work."

"When does this trip come up?"

"Not for another two weeks."

It couldn't be more perfect. Just to make up Maura's mind, he threw in his closing comments. "I'm sure I can arrange to stay here while you're away. That way, if there's any emergency, I'll be on hand to help out."

Jacaranda Meadows was a twenty-minute drive from his office and the apartment he owned at the beach.

Maura's face lit up. "You will? That will really make it easy for Mom and Dad. Bless you, Brady. When you have children, I'll do the same for you. I'm going to tell Jack right away."

Brady smiled as he leaned back and let the hot jets of water pummel the muscles in his back. He was on a roll, and he had St. Patrick to thank for it.

Kate twisted and turned in her narrow cot. Even though she had stuffed her fingers into her ears, she could hear her father swearing. Any minute now he would hit Mama. Helpless tears seeped out of the corners of her eyes. Curling up small didn't help. The sounds of her father's senseless rage whipped through her frame like the winter wind. Cruel, cutting, unavoidable.

Pain carried its own colors. Her father's anger was black, her mother's suffering dirt brown. Kate herself had been the pale yellow of abject fear. Rose, till she had run away with a man who'd callously abandoned her, had been the only bright spot. Rose had been the rich pink of love, of comfort, of reason....

Just when she thought her heart was going to burst, the noise of a car engine racing outside made Kate's eyes fly open.

It took a minute to realize she wasn't in the east Los Angeles tenement that had been home the first nineteen years of her life. In the gray light of dawn, Kate let her gaze rove over each bit of furniture in her bedroom. She was in Jacaranda Meadows. In her own apartment. She was safe here.

It was a while before Kate forced her shaking legs over the side of the bed. She headed for the kitchen. She needed a long, cool drink of water. The nightmare had been occurring more and more frequently lately.

It was brought on by her own tension. All last night, her thoughts had kept wandering back to the man she'd met that afternoon. Brady.

Meeting him had blown a hole in the wall of control around her emotions...something Kate had thought would never happen. In the kitchen, she got a glass and filled it with cool water. Wishing she could feel as excited about Harold hadn't changed a thing. Ordering herself to stop thinking about Brady, a man she would probably never meet again, hadn't worked, either.

Draining the glass, Kate refilled it and carried it to the living room and the rocking chair she had bought at a garage sale. She sat down.

There were other things on her mind, as well. She had counted on her salary from the preschool to pay next semester's college tuition, and now she didn't have a job. After yesterday's expensive purchase, her bank account showed a balance of fifty dollars. She would have to start looking for another job today. It was a good thing she didn't have to pay rent for this apartment.

Keeping the chair in motion, Kate tried to analyze the previous evening. When Harold had kissed her in his mother's house, she hadn't been able to respond. He'd asked her what was wrong and she'd blurted out she was very tired, and would like to go home. Harold had driven her home in silence.

Kate stretched her left hand out. Its bareness was a stern reminder of her failure.

Why couldn't she be a little more enthusiastic about Harold? In the three months she'd known him, she'd discovered he was a really nice person. In addition, he matched every requirement for Mr. Right on her list.

Kate stopped rocking. Her reaction had very little to do with Harold. It was tied to the past she had never told anyone about.

Terrified of being chained to the area she had grown up in, Kate had steered clear of boys in high school. She had dated later, but kissing was as far as she went. An expert at avoiding physical intimacy, Kate had made up a fictitious boyfriend. Her ploy had prevented her being labeled as strange or frigid by her fellow classmates.

Trying to build a good life on the ashes of her childhood wasn't easy. Embers still lurked in those ashes, ready to burst into flame and burn her seriously if she let them.

At sixteen, she had taken a job in a department store in Whittier. The bus trip to work and back each way hadn't bothered her. Working in a good area had been the first step on her journey out of east Los Angeles.

Saving every penny she could, Kate had found an apartment close to the store, soon after her nineteenth birthday. Mama had died there two years later, happy one of her daughters was on her way up.

After Mama's death, Kate had worked harder than ever. It was as if by being successful she could make up to Mama and Rose for all their pain and suffering.

Kate raised her hands to her cheeks, impatiently knuckling aside the tears she had been unaware she was shedding.

Self-pity was no use. Life dealt the cards and one played them to the best of one's ability. Kate intended to use every advantage she could to end up a winner.

She would call Harold later, and offer to take him to that movie he had wanted to see. He would like that.

Kate heard the telephone while she was in the shower. Grabbing a towel, she wrapped it toga-style around herself and hurried into the living room.

''Hello?''

She knew very few people who would call her at this hour of the morning.

''This is Brady. We met at Bernie's yesterday.''

The picture of bold eyes in a craggy face, topped off with wavy hair, immediately imprinted itself on Kate's mind.

Though Brady couldn't see her, Kate nodded as she said, ''Of course.''

"I got your telephone number from your check."

"I see." Her heart was racing, for no reason at all.

"Henrietta mentioned something yesterday about you having your days free now...?"

The words were a tactful substitute for *out-of-work.* "Yes."

"Can you help me out for a few weeks?"

"What did you have in mind?" asked Kate cautiously. Was he offering her a job at Bernie's?

"It's Cody—my four-year-old nephew. My sister has this chance to accompany her husband on a business trip to Australia and New Zealand, but their itinerary will be too hectic for him. My mom and dad can take care of him at night, but my mom works during the day. Could you watch Cody during the day?"

Kate's eyes widened as Brady mentioned the sum his sister was willing to pay her. It was very generous, and the job seemed like the perfect solution to her problems.

"Where would I be watching him?"

Belatedly she remembered caution. She didn't want to run the risk of bumping into Brady every day.

"My sister has a condominium in Amber Court. Do you know where that is?"

"Yes." Amber Court was the only condominium complex in Jacaranda Meadows. It was close to the shopping center.

"Maura feels Cody will be happiest in familiar surroundings, with all his toys and books, during the day."

"I agree."

"For the first meeting, though, I thought we might get together in the park this evening, if that's convenient for you. I'll bring a picnic, and you and Cody can get to know each other. The poor fellow's been through a great deal lately, what with the move from Colorado, and the chicken pox. He had a ear infection after that, and his pediatrician doesn't want him in a preschool setting yet. Says it's too easy for Cody to pick up something else at this stage. My sister won't go with my brother-in-law if she can't find the right person to take care of Cody."

"I know how hard that can be," Kate said quietly, her heart warming to Brady, no matter how she tried to control it. Brady seemed very knowledgeable about his nephew. Most single men were vague about family matters.

"If all goes well this evening, you and my sister could get together tomorrow and discuss other details."

Kate knew what he was saying. *If* Cody likes you. She didn't resent it, was in fact glad to hear it. It was important for parents to listen to their children's opinions of the people who watched over them. Apparently Brady and Cody's parents knew this, too.

"Has Cody had any previous problems with babysitters?"

Brady sounded evasive as he said, "He's an active child and it's awfully hard on him when a baby-sitter expects him to be good and play with his toys so she can watch television. You're different, though. Cody's going to love you."

Kate blushed. One hand clutched the towel as if she were afraid Brady could see her. His voice over the telephone sounded warm and friendly. Too warm. Too friendly.

"I'm free this evening." She wasn't really passing up an evening with Harold for Brady. She was looking into a job opportunity. "I'll bring the names and numbers of a few people your sister can call for references."

"Shall we meet at six, by the swing sets?"

"At six," Kate echoed.

"Well . . . goodbye, then."

"Bye."

"Take care."

Kate replaced the receiver and stared at it.

"Never trust a smooth-talking man," Mama had always said. "Never trust love, either. It'll blind you, so you can't see the truth, till it's too late."

Her life wasn't going to be a rerun of her mother's, or her sister's. Life hadn't given either Mama or Rose a second chance to correct the mistakes they'd made, proving some people never got more than one. Kate couldn't risk blowing her first.

Unwrapping the towel from around her, Kate walked back to the bathroom.

In spite of her thoughts, the mirror showed a face that looked flushed, and there was a shine in her eyes that had something to do with the way Brady had said, "Take care."

The man must have a degree in transmitting charm.

Picking up a hairbrush, Kate began to run it through her hair. She smiled at her reflection. For the first time today, a ray of hope shone through the cloud she had woken up under.

The park was a huge grassy oval in the center of Jacaranda Meadows, surrounded by a tree-lined concrete path ideal for walking or jogging.

The picnic benches and playground equipment were at one end. Cody let go of Brady's hand and headed straight for the swings. At this time of day, the place was deserted. Brady sat down on a nearby bench where he could keep an eye on Cody, while waiting for Kate.

His eyes narrowed as he spotted her park her car and walk toward the play area. Her hair, he noted immediately, was braided and wrapped coronetlike around her head. It made her look even taller, and more graceful than ever. The aqua shirt and black jeans she wore did her perfect figure credit.

In the past twenty-four hours Brady had tried to remind himself lawyers never trusted feelings. They worked with facts. And he couldn't ignore the reality that there was steel at the core of this woman coming toward him. Determined, strong, inflexible steel.

"Hi!"

The shy smile, the quick flash of her dimples, knocked all logic out of Brady's head.

"Hi!" His pulse sped up as if he'd been running, not sitting.

"Is that Cody?" She turned to look at the little boy, and Brady let his gaze linger on her face.

"Yes."

Cody stopped the swing and rushed toward them. Kate took a deep breath, watching as Brady got up. She'd forgotten how that intense look of Brady's seemed to penetrate the very depths of her soul. One minute with him and she was becoming confused again.

"Cody, this is Kate Langdon, the friend I told you about. Kate, this is Cody, my nephew."

Kate took one look at Cody's dark eyes filled with anxiety, and put a hand out. "Hi, Cody."

The little boy shook her hand, looking shy. "Hi!"

Standing close beside his uncle, he stared at her.

"Do you like the park?" Kate asked.

"Yes."

Kate saw one small hand slip into Brady's.

"I love coming here," she told Cody. "I walk here in the mornings and listen to the birds singing. Sometimes

I'm all alone, and I sit on the swings and pump till I go really high and I can see the roofs of the houses.''

Brady sensed Cody relax beside him. She'd said exactly the right things. He watched Kate closely, but there was nothing about her to suggest she was putting on an act.

"Can I go play some more, Uncle Brady?" Cody asked.

"A little while more, and then we'll eat." Brady wanted to find out how Kate's date had gone.

As Cody ran off, Brady pointed to the bench. "Let's sit down."

Kate sat, thinking he meant to fill her in on Cody. The little boy looked normal enough. With her preschool experience, she could pick out the problem kids right away. He wouldn't be any trouble.

"How did last night go?" Brady asked casually. A quick check of her left hand had shown no ring there, yet.

The way Kate's face blazed with color surprised Brady. For a minute he thought she was going to tell him to mind his own business.

"I don't want to talk about it."

The unhappy words tore at him. "What happened?"

"Nothing, really."

"Why don't you tell me what went wrong? Maybe I can help?" Brady tried to sound like a friendly uncle.

Maybe he could at that. Kate looked at him. Brady probably had plenty of experience with women. He might tell her how to get over her nerves when it came to the serious stuff. And he was so easy to talk to.

The quickly controlled tremble of the full lower lip before she bit down on it made Brady tense. "Harold and I just don't seem to be . . . er . . . compatible."

"What do you mean?" She wanted money. Harold evidently had it. What was incompatible about that?

"You know."

The color under her skin, the way she avoided his eyes, gave him a clue.

"You mean the physical side of things isn't working?" What was wrong with this Benson guy, anyway? If Brady had a girl who looked like Kate, there would certainly be no problems on *his* end!

"It isn't anything to do with Harold. It's me." The miserable confession was accompanied by deepening color in her face. She still wouldn't look at him.

"There's nothing wrong with you."

Kate looked at Brady. He sounded very fierce. Which was strange, but not as strange as her compulsion to tell Brady things about herself she had never imagined discussing with anyone.

"Uncle Brady, will you push me on the swings now?"

They both turned to look at Cody.

"Later," Brady said. "Let's eat first and then I'll push both you and Kate on the swings."

Kate's breath caught in her throat at the warm promise of Brady's words. Cody sat beside his uncle and stared at Kate, while Brady took out fast-food containers from a brown paper bag. For a few moments there was silence as they all dug in.

"I'm going to be five in August and I don't take naps anymore," Cody announced, glancing at his uncle for support.

"I don't see why you should have to," Kate said mildly. "Some of the four-year-olds in my class don't sleep in the afternoons. They lie on their mats and read, while the others sleep. A rest is as good as a nap."

Cody considered that seriously, his head tilted to one side, before he asked, "Can you swim?"

"Yes."

She had taken swimming lessons in between dancing lessons and French lessons. Kate had always picked the free classes offered by the local community college. Besides, when you had no money, state and federal aid for education was almost unlimited. America was the only country in the world where people couldn't claim poverty or lack of opportunity as reasons for not being educated.

"My dad says I can swim every day, if you'll be in the pool with me."

"That sounds like the thing to do in this weather," agreed Kate.

Cody grinned at her and Kate knew she'd passed some secret test. The little boy's line of questioning reminded her of Brady's. He, too, had a knack for getting straight to the point.

"Can I have another cookie, Uncle Brady?"

"May I," corrected Brady automatically, handing him one.

"May I," repeated Cody obediently, grinning at Kate.

"I'm sorry he put you through the third degree," Brady apologized, after Cody finished eating and ran off to play. Kate noticed there were a couple more children at the swing sets now.

"I don't mind. Cody seems really intelligent and I'm glad he shared his concerns with me."

"You have a touch of mustard at the corner of your mouth."

As if it were the most natural thing in the world to do, Brady picked up a napkin and wiped her mouth.

Sensation exploded inside Kate as she gripped Brady's hand to stop him. Her breath caught in her lungs. Brady's gaze clashed with hers, and she felt her heart twist in her chest. Under her hand, Brady's felt strong and very male. The scent of his tangy cologne added to her confused state. Cody's laughter in the distance broke the spell.

"Thanks," Kate said awkwardly, withdrawing her hand.

"Maura said she'll call and set up a meeting with you tomorrow, if that's all right."

"Sure. When do they plan to leave?"

"In two weeks, if all goes well."

That should give her time to do something about Harold, Kate decided.

"I was thinking about you and Harold," Brady began, as if he'd tuned in to her thoughts. "Maybe I could help."

"How?"

Brady cleared his throat. "I have some experience in these matters."

"You do?" Was he teasing her?

"Ask my sister," said Brady solemnly. "She and Jack, my brother-in-law, would never have made it to the altar if it hadn't been for me. All a couple needs to untangle the confusion sometimes is some plain talking." Brady hoped Kate didn't watch the same television shows he did. A priest had used those exact words on a show just last week. "You're going to help with Cody. The least I can do is help you with Harold."

"I'm being paid to watch Cody," Kate pointed out.

"I still think it's very nice of you to offer to take this on at such short notice. Not many people would be willing to do that."

Brady observed the struggle in Kate's eyes. The setting sun filtered through the jacaranda tree they were sitting under, turning her hair to mahogany. Idly, Brady wondered if she had a temper to match. Except for the nervousness she had revealed the first day, Kate Langdon was too controlled. Brady had seen that stiff-upper-lip-and-pretend-all's-well facade in so many of his clients before. She discarded it around Cody, but not around him. Brady intended to find out what had happened to make Kate Langdon hide herself behind that too-formal exterior.

"I can help you, Kate," Brady repeated.

"How?"

Kate couldn't believe she and Brady were having this discussion about her personal life.

Brady glanced at the swing set. He didn't know how. Not yet, anyway. "It's going to take some planning, and I can tell Cody's getting tired. Why don't I pick you up tomorrow at five, and we'll go out to dinner and talk?"

Kate stared at him. Did Brady really think he could help her?

"I have to go and push that nephew of mine on the swing as I promised, before he'll leave this place. Coming?"

Kate looked at the hand stretched out to her. Tentatively, she put her own in it. Warmth and strength surrounded her. A slight tug had her on her feet. Brady refused to let her hand go as they walked to the play area.

The fact that she had eaten too much, Kate told herself, must account for the placid state of mind she was in. And for the fact that she'd confided in Brady so much, had actually placed her hand in his. She didn't withdraw her hand from Brady's, but she couldn't ignore the way his touch made her feel.

Hot, bothered, happy.

Chapter Three

Brady's hand against the small of her back, as he escorted her to their table, made Kate feel hot all over. The image of him in a burgundy silk shirt and black slacks was imprinted on her mind. This close to him, the spicy scent of his cologne numbed her senses. She should never have agreed to have dinner with him!

Going out with Brady wasn't the best way to keep her feelings under control. Wishing she'd had his telephone number so she could call him and tell him she had changed her mind about going out with him, hadn't done any good. The fact she *didn't* know his telephone number only proved she didn't think rationally when he was around.

"You look beautiful." Brady's gaze was a lasso rendering her willpower useless. It traveled over her face, and then down to the emerald-green silk jumpsuit she wore.

"Thank you."

Once they were seated, Kate looked around the exclusive restaurant and her heart sank.

"Brady, we don't have to eat here," she whispered, as soon as their waiter had handed them their menus, taken their drink order and left.

"Why not?" He looked surprised. "Doesn't the menu have anything you like?"

Kate closed her eyes in exasperation. It wasn't the menu she didn't like. "It's too expensive," she said, her mind on the exorbitant prices she'd been looking at.

"Don't worry about that. I can afford it," Brady said.

"On your salary?" Kate didn't bother to hide her surprise. "Brady, it's not as if I'm your girlfriend or anything like that. You don't have to impress me."

"Of course not." The answer came out too pat. The smile that accompanied the words made her heart jump.

Kate glared at him. "So, shall we leave right after our drinks?"

"Stop worrying, Kate. I said I can afford it."

Her heart sank at the note of finality in his voice. As the waiter returned and poured sparkling cider into their wineglasses, Kate stared out of the floor-to-ceiling window.

The fact that the maître d' and the waiter had greeted him by name told her Brady was a regular customer here. He had very expensive tastes...just like her father, Chuck Langdon. She sighed inwardly. A man who spent beyond his means was definitely Mr. Wrong as far as Kate was concerned.

And it wasn't only Brady's taste in restaurants that she recognized as expensive. Having worked in the men's section of a department store for years, with one glance Kate could price what Brady wore. The figure she came up with didn't match what she knew salespeople made.

"How did the meeting with Maura go?"

Brady's question forced her to look at him again.

"Very well." She had met Maura and Jack Brigham that morning. The young couple, obviously well-off, had moved from Colorado to be near Maura's parents. They had bought a house, still under construction, in Jacaranda Meadows and were renting the condo they were in now, till May.

"I met your mother, too."

Brady tensed. Sometimes Mom liked boasting about her children's accomplishments.... Had she said anything about his—

"She was in a hurry, so she couldn't stay long."

Brady breathed a sigh of relief. He'd have to think up a good reason to tell his family why he didn't want them mentioning to Kate what he really did for a living. Soon.

"Maura offered me the job, and I accepted. I'm going to go over to the condo every afternoon in the next two weeks to get to know Cody. Thank you for recommending me to Maura, Brady."

"It was nothing. By the way, Maura told me you refused to take any money for these visits you plan." It had been another odd bit that didn't fit into the picture of Kate she'd given him. And even though he hadn't wanted to let on that his sister had spoken to him about the interview, he had to ask. If money was so important, why would she turn any down?

"Getting to know Cody can hardly be called work. I can't take money for that."

Okay. But he'd thought up another little test. He was eager to see what her reaction would be. Carefully, he began, "A lawyer friend of mine is looking for an office assistant. I recommended you and told Juan you'd be available in eight weeks. He's willing to give you insurance and medical benefits, as well as three weeks' leave in summer. He'll pay you well.''

The sum Brady named as her salary worked out to more than what she'd make in three months as a pre-school teacher.

"What does the job entail?" she asked cautiously.

"Answering the telephone, some typing and filing—nothing very difficult.''

A waiter materialized beside them and asked if they were ready to order. Brady didn't like the fact Katie ignored his attempts to get her to try the house special-ity—steak and lobster—and ordered a salad, a chicken sandwich and fries. The thought she was trying to save him money tied Brady up in knots of guilt. The women he'd gone out with in the past believed in getting the best. Lying about what he really did for a living was becoming harder with each passing minute.

Kate didn't seem inclined to return to their earlier dis-cussion. Brady shot her a glance and asked, "Do you think you might want to give the job a try?''

"I don't think I'm the right person for the job, Brady, but thanks.''

"Why not? The money's enough, isn't it?''

"I want to be a teacher, not an office assistant,'' said Kate.

Brady frowned. Why wasn't she interested in making more money for herself?

"If you took the job with Juan, you could take some courses in the evening and become a paralegal eventu-ally. Some of them earn a great deal.''

The sum he mentioned made Kate's eyes widen.

"I want to be a teacher,'' she repeated.

"I just suggested it because you mentioned money's so important to you. Besides, you'll meet more eligible men in a corporate law office, than working in a preschool. Successful lawyers, rich businessmen."

She deserved that, but the words still hurt. Brady made it sound as if she was obsessed with money. Picking up her wineglass, Kate took a sip. How did one explain that she didn't want a filthy rich husband, just someone financially secure and with the right attitude regarding work? Where she'd grown up, most middle-class families had been considered rich—which was enough for her.

Brady cursed himself. Now he'd gone and done it. It was that temper of his, the impatience he couldn't keep harnessed. Brady's only excuse was that he wanted Kate for himself. A part of him wanted to prove Katie really wasn't as mercenary as she thought she was. The flash of pain in her eyes, when he'd made his last statement, made him wish he could kick himself. He had to backtrack quickly.

As the waiter placed their dinner salads in front of them, Brady said, "I'm sorry, Kate. I didn't meant to get so personal."

Deliberately he talked of Cody's exploits for a while, waiting till he sensed her relax, before saying, "Let's get back to the real reason we're here. Have you seen Harold again since his birthday?"

Kate blinked. Harold? She hadn't even thought of him from the moment Brady had picked her up at her apartment.

"What is it about Harold that scares you?"

"N-nothing. I told you, it's not him . . . it's me."

Brady frowned. Why was Kate so positive the trouble lay with her? "How did you and Harold meet?"

"He owns the preschool building. He came in one day when the director wasn't there. I showed him the carpeting we needed replaced, and he asked me out to dinner."

Her voice indicated it had all been about as exciting as a seven-day diet of plain tuna.

Trying to keep his voice noncommittal, Brady said, "Let's start with Sunday night. Name one of the things that bothered you the most."

The fact that I couldn't respond to Harold.

Would Brady really know something that might help her? His manner, and the way he was around her, told Kate he had plenty of experience with women. He might be the right one to know what a man liked best in a woman. Intuition warned her that if she carried on as she'd done in the past, she was going to lose Harold. It wouldn't be easy to find someone else like him. Harold was hardworking, reasonably well-off and ambitious. All three were good sound traits in a man.

"I...I can't seem to warm up to the physical side of our relationship." Watching Brady lift a brow, Kate said quickly, "Harold is very sweet.... It's just me. I think there's something wrong with my hormones."

Brady lifted his wineglass to his lips to hide his smile. He'd bet a year's salary there was nothing wrong with Katie.

"Why don't you call Harold and suggest he take you somewhere romantic for a weekend?"

Kate's face blanched. "G-go away together?"

Brady hid his grin behind a napkin. Kate looked as thrilled as if he'd suggested another seven days on the tuna diet.

"Yes. Buy yourself some really pretty lingerie. Romantic surroundings can make a real difference. Have you discussed your fears about being unresponsive with Harold?"

Kate's face flamed. "No!"

The sharp retort pleased Brady very much. There was hope for him yet. He picked up his wineglass again.

"I mean, I'm not into that sort of thing," Kate amended.

"What sort of thing?" He wanted to let out the war whoop he and Cody had perfected in his parents' backyard last week, but controlled himself.

"Going to bed with a man before I'm married to him."

"People in love do it all the time these days," Brady pointed out.

"Well, I don't." Kate turned her face away from him.

Brady curbed his impulse to get up and perform the Irish jig right there in the restaurant. This was going even better than he could have hoped. "Kate, I don't think you've thought this marriage thing through properly."

"What do you mean?"

"It's normal to be in love with the person you're planning to marry. Enjoy touching him and being touched by him. I only suggested going away with Harold, because in a different setting you might relax."

"That won't work for me," Kate said coolly. "I don't believe in love. Emotion blinds you and that's the reason there are so many unhappy marriages around these days. People wake up too late to discover they have nothing in common with the person they've married."

"You're talking about infatuation, not love," Brady pointed out.

"What's the difference?" Kate demanded. "They're both a state in which a person doesn't think rationally."

She made love sound like a virus to be avoided.

"What's your criterion for marriage?" Brady demanded.

"A couple should have common interests. Harold and I are both ambitious. We share the same dreams of success."

"Don't forget wealth," added Brady bitterly. He cursed inwardly. He had simply let her beauty blind him to her real nature. Kate Langdon was no different from the women who threw themselves at him once they discovered how rich he was. How could he have been so wrong?

For an instant Brady thought he saw a shadow of pain in Kate's eyes, but she didn't look away. "Money is probably the most important of all."

He had to hand it to her. At least she was honest about her motives.

"Why?" Brady demanded, angrier than he had been in a long time.

"Money provides security," he heard Kate say. "Once you have that as a foundation, love will grow."

"Is that what you think of when Harold kisses you?" Brady demanded. "How rich you'll be when he marries you?"

Kate flushed. "Of course not."

"Then why is money so important?"

"I told you. It provides security. Children need security."

Brady's jaw clenched. There had to be a connection in Kate's mind for her to have jumped from discussing marriage to children. The only answer he could think of disturbed him.

"Were you poor growing up, Kate?"

She lifted her drink and took a sip before saying, "Yes."

The hand that traced a pattern on the lace tablecloth shook slightly.

"You have to think about yourself before you think of the kids you may or may not have. There's more to marriage than providing security for your children."

Kate opened her mouth to say something, but Brady wasn't finished. "There's caring and loving and wanting to be with the other person so badly, it hurts to imagine life without them. You'll wither in a cold relationship. Marrying without love will be the biggest mistake you've ever made."

Brady's best friend, Pete Shroff, was a divorce lawyer. The cases he discussed clearly illustrated most people married for the wrong reasons: power, prestige, sheer physical attraction. A marriage wasn't easy to undo. Brady tried tackling the issue from a different perspective.

"What does *Harold* want? He might have his own blueprint and it might include love, you know. Have you told him how you feel about the emotion?"

"No."

Her stiff answer didn't stop Brady. "Marriage, in case you didn't know, involves close encounters of the personal kind on a daily basis."

The fact was one Kate struggled with after every date with Harold. Hearing the words out loud made them impossible to hide from any longer. Covering fear with anger, she said through clenched teeth, "That's my business. I thought you were going to help, not take my life over."

Brady was at the end of his short fuse again. "What happens when you meet someone you really like? Do you check them off against your list and then disqualify them if they aren't rich and ambitious?"

"Can we leave now?" Kate asked politely. There was no point in prolonging this conversation. Brady would never understand. Not if she explained it to him for a million years. She didn't know why she had ever thought him easy to talk to.

"Of course. I'm sorry if I upset you by voicing some of my own convictions. I only thought a frank discussion would help you discover what's holding you and Harold back from making a final commitment."

The shuttered look on her face told him he had to do some fast talking. Would she buy his excuse? Brady wondered if it was too late to recover lost ground. He had to keep the channels of communication between him and Katie open. It was the only way he'd be able to keep track of her relationship with Harold.

A part of him was glad he'd got his message across, though he felt guilty about treating her as if she were a witness he was cross-examining. Katie's determination to marry for financial security made him want to reach out and shake her.

As he paid for their meal with a credit card, and watched Katie, Brady told himself he had made absolutely no headway tonight. He'd hoped that the dinner and spending time with him would give Katie a chance to get to know him better. Make her realize the importance of the chemistry between them. His impatience had ruined everything. Katie looked as if she never wanted to see him again.

Kate tried to ignore the pain in her heart as they drove home in silence. It shouldn't matter that Brady thought she was greedy and selfish. She had to remember that the most important thing in life was for her to stick to her plan.

Discussing her plans with Brady had unsettled her, not helped her. Kate rubbed the back of her neck to ease the tension knotting there.

It doesn't matter what he thinks of you, pointed out her brain.

It does matter, defended her heart. *I don't want Brady misunderstanding my reasons for marrying a man who can provide me with financial security.*

Brady related with her on a different level to anyone she had known. An intensely personal level. For some reason, it was important that Brady think well of her. But hope of that seemed dismal indeed.

Cody looked up from the picture he was coloring and said, "Mommy's going to be surprised when she comes back and sees the book I've made for her."

"That's right."

Cody drew pictures every day of things they did and Kate filed them in a book titled *Cody's Adventures*. The picture diary was going to be a gift for Maura and Jack Brigham when they returned from their trip.

Kate looked at Cody and sighed. She wished Cody didn't look so much like Brady. She didn't need to be constantly reminded of someone she wanted to relegate to a corner of her mind.

Cody's parents had left Sunday night. Kate had sensed Maura's relief over the fact that Kate got on so well with Cody, and that the youngster was looking forward to the things they planned together. A day at Disneyland, a visit to the zoo, daily swims in the pool.

"He actually keeps asking me how many days till you can come watch him full-time," Maura had told Kate on her third visit. "I'm so grateful you could do this at such short notice. We'll miss Cody terribly, but we're not worried about leaving him anymore. Between you, Brady and my parents, Cody's going to be well cared for."

Cody's grandparents had invited Kate to their beautiful home for dinner one night. The senior Gallaghers were obviously well-to-do, and Kate had wondered if that was why Brady was content with being a salesman. Did his parents pay most of his bills for him?

The thought had been another red flag. Chuck Langdon had depended on his wealthy parents to support him. He had never thought they would throw him out when he insisted on marrying the chauffeur's daughter. It had been impossible for her father to develop good work habits, or curtail his expensive ones.

Seeing the Gallaghers together, Kate had realized how close-knit they were. It was obvious Brady and Maura had grown up in a loving home. No wonder Brady thought only love mattered in a marriage. She understood his reasoning, but that didn't change her own. No matter how he made her feel physically, her brain insisted he was still Mr. Wrong.

"Kate, stand still, so I can draw you," commanded Cody.

"I hope you're going to make me gorgeous." Kate stopped dusting and struck a pose, making Cody giggle.

Kate had told Mrs. Gallagher that she would give her a daily telephone report each night. So far, everything had gone well these past two days. The next instant Kate amended that to *almost* everything.

She hadn't realized how often she would be seeing Brady once she took this job. Brady seemed to turn up everywhere in the past two weeks. He'd spent an afternoon at the park with her and Cody, an hour another day playing card games with them. He'd even been at his parents' place when she'd gone there for dinner. Though the only comments they exchanged were casual, and his manner was nothing but friendly, Kate couldn't stop the way she reacted to him. Her senses rioted, her body melted and her mind turned to slush. Around him she felt as fragile as glass.

Now he dropped off and picked up Cody every day, taking time to linger for a good fifteen minutes each morning. On the pretext of asking about Cody's day, he usually talked to her in the evenings, as well. She found no fault with his manner, but his eyes were a different matter. They conveyed a deep and scary message, one that hinted Brady was as aware as her that things would never be normal between them.

Kate couldn't understand why Brady had such an effect on her. What was so special about him? So, okay, he topped her by a couple of inches. Well, maybe a bit more than that. And till she met him, Kate *had* told herself she liked very tall men. Now it seemed that it didn't matter whether Brady was tall or short.

The memory of how Brady had looked just that morning when he'd dropped Cody off at the condominium, flashed into Kate's mind. He had filled the pristine white shirt he wore with gray slacks, very nicely. A silk tie drew attention to his know-it-all eyes. The strength of him came across in his clean-shaven face, the firm lips, the line of his jaw. He had smiled at her, and Kate's emotions had erupted into a frenzy of awareness. His gaze had skimmed her, as it always did, from head to foot and she'd blushed as his warm voice had said, "Have a nice day."

A commonplace remark that had made her feel uncommonly breathless. It proved Brady had some kind of direct line to her senses.

"You can look now."

Kate moved to Cody's side and stared at the matchstick figure with a pumpkin head and a feather duster in one hand. "Looks just like me."

"Uncle Brady says you're very pretty, so I made you pretty," Cody stated happily.

"Uncle Brady said that?" A pulse started beating at the base of Kate's throat.

"I heard him tell Grandma."

Twice a week, when Kate had to go to college, Brady picked Cody up at three. According to Cody, Brady stayed and played with him till Grandma and Grandpa got back. Kate had asked if Brady lived with them, and Cody had said yes.

She could understand why Brady would have to live with his parents. The hours he worked must barely pay for his expensive tastes. He obviously couldn't be saving a dime of his salary. Did Brady know inheritances had terms and conditions attached to them? For his own sake, a man had to be able to support his needs.

Brady may not have much going for him, but he beats any man you've ever known, hands down, when it comes to being charming, her heart insisted.

He's Chuck Langdon all over again, warned her brain.

Maybe, but he makes you feel alive. Have you ever felt this way around anyone else? With Brady, you're always smiling.

Kate raised her fingers to her lips. That was true. When she was with Brady, she forgot the blueprint she had drawn up.

"I'm going to build a tower up to the sky now," Cody boasted, stuffing his crayons back into their box.

"Good idea," Kate said, watching him drag the laundry basket, which held an assortment of blocks, out of the huge closet in the family room.

As she passed Cody the blocks he requested, Kate's thoughts went back to Brady. It was impossible to avoid him, so the only thing to do was exercise more control over herself.

Mama had once felt the way Kate did now. Rose, too. Charmed off their feet, they had woken too late to do anything about the mess they'd found themselves in.

"A lifetime," Mama had told Kate and Rose once, "is a long time to pay for a single mistake. Don't you girls let any man turn your head with his smooth talk."

The fact that Rose had forgotten was all the more reason for Kate to remember.

"Why are you crying, Kate? Are you sad?"

Startled, Kate realized a tear was trailing down her cheek. Jumping up from the carpet where she had been sitting cross-legged, she said, "I think I've got a lash in my eye. I'd better wash it out."

The doorbell rang, startling Kate. A quick glance at the clock on the wall showed it was ten minutes to three.

"Kate's got an eyelash in her eye. Can you make it go away?"

Kate groaned to herself as she heard the sentence Cody greeted Brady with.

"Let's take a look."

He put his briefcase down and came toward her. "Which eye is it, Kate?"

"The left," she said, rubbing it furiously. "I think the eyelash is out now."

"Let me make sure."

His warm touch startled her as he cupped her face and tilted it upward, turning it toward the window. This close to him, she felt strangely weak. Kate shut her eyes.

"I'm just going to take a look."

She felt his thumb and forefinger open her left eye gently. His breath, warm and peppermint fresh, made her tense. Inches separated them and the sudden surge of need to close the gap took Kate unawares.

"Can you find it?" Cody demanded beside them.

"Kate's right. There's nothing in there now, buddy," Brady said.

"Blow in her eye," Cody advised. "That's what Mommy does when I have something in my eye."

"There's no need...." Kate's voice trailed away as she realized Brady had no intention of letting her go.

She felt him take a deep breath, felt its gentle warmth as he blew into her eye.

The weakness in her head spread to her legs. Yanking herself away, she said, "I'm fine now. I've got to rush or I'll be late for my class. Bye, Brady. Bye, Cody."

Grabbing her bag, Kate left the condominium without a backward look. It took a while for her pulse to return to normal.

Brady took out a brief he had picked up at the office that morning. He may as well review it, he decided, while Cody watched his favorite cartoons.

"Did you have a good time today?" he asked.

Talking to Cody about his day told Brady a great deal about Kate. He'd been unusually patient since his first meeting with Kate. These last two weeks hadn't been easy, for a number of reasons.

Every time he saw Katie, the conviction that they were meant for each other deepened. The main reason he'd held back was that he'd wanted to make up for his blunders the night he'd taken her out to dinner. The thought that he'd hurt Katie had bothered him immensely and he'd forced himself to give her time to get used to him.

He'd seen her watching him when she thought no one else was looking. Her wariness told him that getting her to trust him meant simply being around without putting any kind of pressure on her.

Two weeks of the slow pace was enough. As far as Brady was concerned, the waiting was over. From now on, he intended to go full steam ahead with his plans. He was going to win Katie over to his way of thinking, as soon as possible. And Harold Benson be damned.

"Kate and I went for a swim and she showed me how to lie on my back 'n float. I played with Jenny from next door in the sand pit. Then I had a shower and Kate 'n me made macaroni and cheese for lunch. Kate told me two stories. Then I fell asleep. Kate says it's not because I'm a baby. She says swimming makes everyone sleepy."

"That's right, buddy. Even I fall asleep after a swim sometimes."

"We're going to the zoo on Friday, because Kate doesn't have school that day."

Brady tensed. At last, some real information!

"Oh?"

"Kate says we can take a picnic lunch and eat before we walk around and see the lellephants, the tigers, the monkeys, everything." Cody stared at him and then said, "You want to come and see the animals, too, Uncle Brady?"

Brady smiled at his nephew. "Sounds like a great idea."

The grin didn't leave his face as Cody moved away and switched on the television. His luck was holding. With a little Irish tenacity, he would soon change Katie's mind for her.

Kate frowned at the telephone when it rang at eight that night. She had finished talking with Mrs Gallagher half an hour ago, and she wasn't expecting any other calls.

Her face buried under a layer of a frog-green facial mask guaranteed to firm, tone and replenish, she reached for the receiver.

"Kate, it's me, Brady." The warm voice that came over the wire in response to her "hello," made Kate jump.

"Yes?" Her throat suddenly felt coated with the same clay mask she had used on her face.

"Cody invited me to go along to the zoo with you on Friday."

Kate closed her eyes. Oh, Cody!

"My mom's a little concerned about your car, as well, which is why I accepted Cody's invitation."

Kate bit her lip. She'd had an awful time starting the old Ford once when Mr. and Mrs. Gallagher had been at the Brighams' condominium, and they'd all come out to ask if she needed help. Brady had jump-started the car again for her. She'd had the car tuned up since, but she could see how it might concern the Gallaghers to have her drive their grandson to the zoo in it.

"Kate? Are you still there?"

"I'm still here, Brady. If you're sure you want to come along, we plan to leave Friday around eleven-thirty."

"I'm looking forward to it," Brady said smoothly. "By the way, how are you doing with Harold?"

If the stuff on her face hadn't hardened so much, Kate's brows would have flown up. She hadn't even thought of Harold for some time.

"He . . . he's fine."

"Just wanted to check on your progress and see if there's anything I can do to help. If you'd like to go out for another discussion, just say the word. We all appreciate everything you're doing with Cody. I promised to help you with Harold, and I'm a man of my word.''

I'll just bet you are, Kate thought, recalling the tempest he'd aroused in her the last time he'd ''helped'' with Harold.

''Actually, your talk did do some good, Brady,'' Kate found herself saying quickly. Suddenly it was imperative to widen the narrowing distance between Brady and herself. ''Harold and I are talking more and it's helping us.''

''I see.'' Brady's voice sounded dangerously quiet. ''I'm glad things are working out the way you want them to. Good night, Kate.''

She stared at her reflection in the mirror of her dresser.

Why did you lie to Brady? her heart demanded. *You haven't seen Harold since his birthday.*

You had to lie to protect yourself, appeased her brain. *Brady's too dangerous for you.*

From the mirror, her face, frozen in the hardening mask, looked back at her. Only her eyes, blazing pinpoints of accusation, conveyed that she had broken her most important rule of always being honest.

It was all Brady's fault.

Chapter Four

"He said to 'mind you he's goin' to be here soon to take us to the zoo. We're goin' to have a picnic first, then see the animals."

Kate looked at Cody's upturned face, a feeling of unease overtaking her. This was the first time Brady had dropped Cody off without coming in to say hello.

It was all for the best, Kate told herself fiercely.

Smiling at Cody, she took the backpack he held. "We'd better get started with the brownies, then, or they won't be ready to take along."

Brady managed to get a great deal of time off work, Kate thought as she measured ingredients into a bowl. She hoped he wasn't jeopardizing his job to spend time with them.

His casual attitude to work was yet another red flag, warning her to be careful.

Cody pulled a chair to the counter and stood on it, wooden spoon in hand, watching her measure the ingredients the recipe called for. "I'm going to mix it for you. Round 'n round 'n round."

"Slowly," Kate cautioned, holding the plastic bowl so that Cody wouldn't sweep it off the counter with his enthusiasm for mixing.

Her heart twisted at the thought that Brady didn't like the fact she was seeing Harold. Even if she wasn't, it was nobody's business but her own. She couldn't encourage Brady, not when he was so clearly Mr. Wrong.

"Can I stop mixing? My arm hurts."

Startled, Kate looked at Cody. Guilt, because she'd let him mix for so long, colored her face as she said, "I bet these are going to be the best brownies ever. Let me pour the batter into the pan, and I'll let you have the bowl to lick."

"Do you think there'll be enough for Grandma and Grandpa?" Cody asked anxiously. "They like brownies, too."

"Of course."

Aware that Cody was going to have a hard time waiting for Brady, Kate said, "Why don't you find a book for us to read, while I put these in the oven? We can make the sandwiches later."

The sound of the doorbell at eleven-fifteen made Kate's pulses jump. Cody rushed to the door as she put the last of the sandwiches she'd made into the picnic basket.

"We made some brownies. Wait till you taste 'em. We've got enough for Grandma and Grandpa too."

Hanging on to Brady's arm, Cody chattered nonstop till Brady reached the kitchen counter.

"Hello, Kate."

Kate looked up and almost drowned in the dark eyes watching her. "Hi, Brady."

Surely it was her unreliable imagination that suggested there was pain mixed in with the underlying anger in his gaze?

"I'm going to change my shoes and bring my bag down," announced Cody.

Maura had told Kate she always took a change of clothes along for Cody on every outing, just in case of accidents.

"You do that, buddy." Brady picked up a brownie and bit into it. "These are good."

Brady stared at Katie. A quick scan of her left hand showed no sign of a ring yet. So, Harold was still a semifinalist. Brady felt better. He still intended to eliminate the other man's chances with Kate.

He wanted to tell her how nice she looked in pink. Her hair was in its usual coronet and her skin glowed. He had only one complaint. The shorts she had on were long and loose, almost reaching her knees. Brady wished she'd worn the pair he'd seen her in that first day.

He knew better than to say that out loud, though. Confidence was different from ignoring the facts in front of him. Things were different now. The fact that Kate was still seeing Harold erected a barrier between them. So far, Kate had made it very clear that she intended staying behind it for the rest of her life.

She refused to meet his eyes as she pretended the counter needed wiping down one more time. Her actions, the nervous gestures, the flicker in her eyes as she pretended not to see the need in his, told their own story. The clues fanned the spark in the pit of Brady's stomach into an all-consuming flame. Kate was still afraid to acknowledge what was between them.

"Are the brownies from a mix?"

"No. Cody and I made them from scratch. They're much cheaper that way...."

Kate's voice faded. She had to be careful. What she'd just said would only confirm Brady's impression that she was obsessed with money. And, though she still didn't know why it mattered so, it did. Brady's opinion of her mattered.

"Maura and Mom make things from scratch, too. They say there are less additives in our diet that way. I hope you're keeping an account of what you spend."

"I am."

Kate turned to put a few things away and close a kitchen cabinet. She wished her hands would stop shaking. It was ridiculous to behave like this with someone she barely knew. Sunday would make it exactly three weeks since she'd met Brady, hardly long enough for the way he made her feel.

"So, how's it going with Harold?"

Kate stared at the tin of cocoa powder in her hand. Her reaction to Brady when he had come in had shaken her with its intensity. Her heart had threatened to leap out of her chest, and her pulse was still not back to normal. For her own good, she had to continue to widen the distance between them. She used the only weapon she had.

"He's fine. We're going out tomorrow night." The lie came easily, proving everything improved with practice.

Brady glared at her through narrowed eyes. Nervous, Kate wet her lips.

"That's great," snapped Brady, picking up the picnic basket.

Kate put a hand up to cover her mouth as the kitchen door closed. Why on earth had she told Brady another outright lie? Harold had called last night and suggested taking her out for a meal, but she'd told him she had to work on a term paper. She had lied about that, too. Was there such a thing as a professional liar, and how many lies did one tell before one qualified for a certificate?

"I'm ready." Cody raced down the stairs, bag in hand. "Let's go."

Kate picked up her handbag and the keys to the condo. Following Cody out to the BMW, she told herself to stop being silly. Brady was just another man.

She had to concentrate on her plan. Finding Mr. Right, even if Harold wasn't him, might take some time, but it wasn't impossible. In the meantime, all she had to do was steer clear of Mr. Wrong.

The tug on Kate's hand stopped her in front of the chimpanzee cage.

"Look." Cody smiled up at Kate and Brady. He had taken both their hands as they'd begun the tour. "They're like the ones in my book. Can I go to the other side and take a look at the one that's sleepin'?"

"As long as you stay where you can see us, and we can see you," Brady said.

Cody ran a few feet away to get a better look at the baby sleeping in its mother's arms.

"I can see you from here, Uncle Brady," he yelled, as if he were twenty feet away, instead of four.

"That's good, buddy."

Brady stole a glance at Kate's face. Cody's chatter had covered the fact she'd said very little as they'd eaten. Now, as he watched, she lifted her shoulders up as close to her neck as possible and then let them drop.

"What's wrong?"

She hadn't meant to give herself away, but the movement was an automatic way of lessening tension. "It's my neck. It stiffens up from time to time. A physical therapist showed me a few simple exercises to relieve the pain."

Brady put his hand on her neck before she could draw another breath. The thought Kate might be in any sort of pain bothered him. "Let me rub it for you."

Kate stiffened. Brady's hand massaged up a storm inside her. After a few seconds he moved to stand behind her.

"I can do it better this way." He rested both thumbs against her vertebrae, while his splayed fingers cupped her shoulders. Gradually, but firmly, he began to move his thumbs in mind-numbing circles.

Kate closed her eyes. Heat enveloped her, melting her insides like a vanilla fudge sundae left out in the sun. Brady's touch felt so good.

"What's bothering you, Kate?" He could feel the muscles knotted there.

"N-nothing."

He hadn't expected her to tell him. Realizing the best way to relieve her mind of tension was to distract her, he said, "Look at those two go."

They watched two chimps in the cage chase each other, while another one jumped up and down and cheered.

Cody had returned to their side, and was digging in the sand with a stick.

"Cute, aren't they?" Brady said, glad to feel Kate relaxing.

"Very." She turned her head to check on Cody, and Brady allowed his hands to sweep up and down the sides of her neck.

"Do you agree with the theory that chimps are more intelligent than some humans?"

"Is that a fact?" Kate's startled voice reached Brady and it was all he could do not to turn her toward him and kiss her for taking his teasing so seriously. Having his hands on her skin was a sure way to drive himself crazy. Her scent, her nearness, her sweet sexy voice—filled him, making him want more of her.

"It's a fact," said Brady solemnly. "They're so smart that they can do everything Man does, sometimes even better. Everything except go to work, that is. They're too smart to fall into that old trap."

Kate looked down at Cody, still digging in the ground. She felt cold suddenly. Is that how Brady thought of work? As a trap that smart people didn't fall into?

Brady wanted to bite his tongue as he felt her stiffen. He'd said something wrong. Desperate to distract Kate, he said, "I can never figure out if they learn from us, or we learn from them," he said.

"My neck is fine now, thanks."

She was about to move away from him. Brady put his arms around her from the back, holding her within their circle.

"Shh!" he said, placing his face close to hers. "Don't disturb them."

Kate looked straight ahead, wondering what Brady was up to now. In the cage, the two chimps had stopped running and had their arms on each other's shoulders. Even as Kate watched, they bent forward and seriously touched lips.

"Kiss and make up is the best idea that pair has had all day," Brady whispered into her ear.

Kate turned her face to smile at him.

"Monkey see, monkey do!" Brady said promptly, and, turning her around bodily, he brushed his lips against hers.

As far as kisses went, it was a mere introduction of their lips. There was no real reason for Kate's heart to pound. No reason, either, for her to feel as if her insides had melted completely. She put her hands up to Brady's chest to steady herself, and he covered them with his own as he looked into her eyes.

"Uncle Brady, why are you kissin' Kate?" Cody demanded, pushing himself between them. Holding Kate's hand protectively, he looked up at his uncle.

"No reason, buddy," Brady said reassuringly. "Kate's my friend, and sometimes friends kiss."

Cody thought about his uncle's statement for a minute. Then he asked, "Are you going to put a baby in Kate's stomach?"

"What?" The explosion of amazement from Brady was almost a shout. Kate couldn't believe she'd heard what Cody had just said.

"Jenny says her Mom tole her that when grown-ups like each other, they hug and kiss and sometimes the daddy puts a baby in the mommy's stomach. That's how Jenny's mom has a baby in her stomach. Are you going to put a baby in Kate's?"

Brady stared at Cody, wondering how to work his way out of the tangle of reproductive theory in his nephew's head, when he heard Kate say calmly, "Jenny's mommy and daddy are married. They are having a baby because they want to. Your Uncle Brady and I are just friends. Friends kiss just because they like each other, not because they want to have a baby."

Brady watched as Cody thought that over and evidently decided to accept the explanation. "Am I your friend, too, Kate?"

"Of course you are, Cody."

"Can I have a kiss?"

Laughing, Kate bent and kissed Cody on his forehead. Happy, the four-year-old held his other hand out to his uncle. "Let's go see the birds now."

Brady let out a noisy sigh. Things had gotten very awkward there for a while. He stole a glance at Kate. She'd handled a tricky situation very well.

Kate told herself she'd have to monitor Cody's conversations with Jenny, the little girl next door, more closely.

In spite of his unexpected questions, Kate had never been more glad to have Cody along as they walked along the enclosures. His endless questions kept Brady busy, and gave her time to sort herself out. Her lips tingled with the imprint of Brady's lips. Heat poured through her veins. There had been nothing laid-back about her reaction to Brady's kiss.

She shut her eyes briefly, recalling the pressure of that well-shaped mouth on hers. Warm, friendly, casual. There was nothing to frighten her, no suggestion that Brady wanted more.

You're a fool if you don't see how dangerous he is, pointed out her brain.

It was only a friendly kiss, Kate's heart protested. *He would have done the same with anyone else.*

The thought doused the fire his kiss had ignited. Would Brady really have kissed any female who'd been beside him at that moment?

Kate frowned. For some reason the thought irritated her immensely.

"I'm going to take Cody to the water fountain. We're both thirsty. Do you want to come with us?"

Kate looked at Brady blankly for a second, then said, "I'll wait right here, if you don't mind."

Sitting on a convenient bench, Kate stared into the distance.

The kiss was proof that she didn't have her emotions under control. Her lies about seeing Harold hadn't given her any protection when push came to shove.

One brush of Brady's lips and she was ready to go up in smoke.

If he had grabbed her, she would have resisted it, but his mouth had rested against hers gently, coaxing, not demanding a response from her.

For a second, her imagination wondered what would have happened if Brady had deepened the kiss. The way her heart sped up told her she wouldn't have minded.

"Kate, are you taking a nap?"

Her eyes flew open, and her color deepened. "No. I was just thinking."

Over Cody's head, her gaze flew to Brady's. The audacious wink he sent her way told her he could guess what she was thinking about.

Jumping up, Kate grabbed Cody's hand. "Let's hurry," she said, her voice coming out hoarse. "There's so much to see."

"That's right, Kate," Brady confirmed with a smile. "There's so much to see and do yet."

Refusing to look at him, Kate walked down a path that led to the lion enclosure. Were Brady's words, with their double innuendo, a warning? The thought boded ill for her peace of mind.

"Have you ever been in love?" Brady looked moodily at his friend Pete Shroff, over his ham-and-cheese sandwich. Coming in on a Saturday was the only way to catch up on all the time he'd spent away from the office recently.

Brady had known Pete since law school, and now they had offices in the same building. Brady had seen Pete's Jaguar in the parking lot today and had invited his friend to have lunch with him.

Pete looked at him in surprise. "You know I have. Last month I was in love with Rita. Now I'm in love with Cyndi-Lou."

"That's not what I meant," Brady said, irritated by Pete's reference to his constant affairs. They didn't bear comparison to what he felt for Kate. "Aside from your flings, have you ever been in love in a way where you want to get married and take care of someone the rest of your life?"

"Are you coming down with something?" Pete asked in horror. "You sound like my mother."

"Pete, be serious."

"I am serious," said his friend. "I'm a divorce lawyer, Brady. I'm too busy untangling other peoples' messes to want to be in one of my own. Haven't you learned anything from the cases I've discussed with you? Which reminds me—" he glanced at his watch— "I've got another appointment in exactly ten minutes."

Brady stared moodily at Pete's back till his friend disappeared through the swinging doors of the restaurant.

He didn't give a damn what Pete said or thought. He wanted more than just a fling with Kate.

The kiss had been a mistake because it had unleashed a powerful, uncontrollable longing in his chest, one that hurt with every breath he took. Brady wanted to kiss her again, hold her and whisper words of passion against her mouth. The Irish part of him was done with being noble.

Brady crumpled his napkin and threw it on the table. He wasn't going to sit back and let Harold walk away with her.

Sorting the Guthries' mail on Saturday, Kate frowned at the letter in her hand. It was from Arletha Henry, her English teacher in high school. Kate hoped there was nothing wrong with her. She had just visited her old friend last weekend.

Unlocking the door to her apartment, Kate set her grocery bag down on the kitchen counter and ripped open the envelope. The one page letter was brief and to the point.

Mrs. Henry was writing to tell her about one of Kate's classmates. Whitney Rudolph's husband of five years had left her. With two kids to feed, and another on the way, she was desperate. Could Kate help Whitney out in any way?

Kate felt the shaking begin deep inside as she walked over to the writing desk in front of the window. Whitney had been the most popular girl in their class and definitely the prettiest. She'd married right after high school, madly in love.

Instead of Whitney's blue eyes, Kate pictured Rose's green ones as she'd seen them last. They'd held only emptiness; they'd been silent tombstones to all Rose's suffering. Both Whitney and Rose had trusted love, and it hadn't lasted.

Kate looked out of the window, blankly. The gardener had trimmed the hedges. If only the obstacles in life could be removed as easily as overgrown shrubbery.

Kate made out a check, glad her new job enabled her to help Whitney, and wrote a short note to Mrs. Henry. She was still haunted by guilt because she hadn't been able to do anything for Rose. Telling herself there was nothing a scared fifteen-year-old *could* have done, didn't help.

Fighting the deep sadness her sister's memory always brought, Kate walked to the Guthries' mailbox with her letter. The postman would pick it up when he left the mail on Monday. After she closed the mailbox, Kate wrapped her arms around herself.

The reminder had come just in time. Trusting a man who had no interest in working and a devil-may-care attitude was stupid.

She'd been a fool to let Brady get to her yesterday. A fool to forget Mama and Rose. Letting her heart lead her around in this matter was dangerous. She needed to sort out the jumble in her head, and reinforce her original plan with the steel of logic.

Brady's heart did a free-fall when Kate opened the door of the condo Monday morning. She looked absolutely beautiful. Radiant, in fact. The peach jumpsuit she was wearing matched the color of her skin. The tiny brass buttons down the front of her jumpsuit seemed to issue a sensational invitation all their own for Brady to undo them.

He looked away, trying to concentrate on the matter at hand.

"Hi, Kate!" Cody rushed up to his bedroom to check if everything was as he had left it Friday.

Brady stepped into the living room, holding the bag his mother had given him for Kate.

"Interesting weekend?"

She beamed from ear to ear. "Perfect."

His blood turned to ice. "Did you see Harold?" he managed to get out.

Kate nodded.

Brady's eyes narrowed. "And?"

"I took your advice. Harold was delighted when I suggested we go away for a weekend together."

"I see." This is what he got for being so free with his advice. It had boomeranged on him.

"So you still think Harold's the man of your dreams?"

She hadn't been able to afford the luxury of dreams. "I still think financial security is the most important factor in a marriage."

Setting the grocery bag on the counter with a thump, he turned away. "I'm late for work."

The door slammed behind him.

Kate jumped and blinked at the sudden moisture in her eyes. She should be glad her little act had been so successful. Instead, she was left feeling terrible. When she'd thought out her plan, she hadn't counted on the way Brady's face had changed, or the flash of pain in his eyes.

Kate put a hand up to rub her neck. She'd done the right thing. At the store where she'd worked, leather shoes like the pair he had on retailed at over a hundred dollars. As a prod that Brady had very expensive tastes, it was most effective. Indulging his taste for luxuries wasn't a habit that changed in a man. And on a salesman's salary, that left room for only one person.

"What's wrong, Kate? Do you have another eyelash in your eye?"

She looked at Cody. Lifting a finger, she blotted the tear trailing down her cheek. "I did, but it fell out. Let me put the groceries away, and then you can tell me all about your weekend."

Cody made her work fun. As long as she had plenty of things planned to do, the four year old never gave her any trouble. Brady was another matter. Tackling the heavy feeling inside became increasingly difficult in the next three days. Mrs. Gallagher picked Cody up every day, even on Kate's school nights, and when Brady dropped Cody off in the mornings, he didn't get out of the car. He was definitely avoiding her.

Kate told herself she should be glad, not sorry, that she had finally got her message across so clearly. But she wasn't.

When the telephone rang on Thursday at four, Kate answered it and was surprised to hear Mr. Gallagher at the end of the line. "Kate, there's been a family emergency m'dear. Berry's eighty-one-year-old cousin has just been hospitalized with a broken hip. I'm going to drive Berry down to San Diego, right away, to see Ellen. Would it be possible for you to watch Cody tonight? Maura said if there was ever a need, you'd offered to stay overnight."

"Of course," said Kate immediately. "That will be no problem. Don't worry about Cody at all."

"What about those people you house-sit for? Will they mind?"

"Oh, no. They've made it very clear the fact I house-sit doesn't mean I have to spend every single night there. I'll check on things this evening."

As Mr. Gallagher explained things to his grandson, Kate wondered where Brady was. Maybe, she decided, he was going to drive down to San Diego, as well.

"Grandpa says we can spend the night here."

To look at Cody's shining face, one would think he'd just been told he could have two birthdays this year. Kate couldn't help smiling. "That's right."

"You're going to sleep in Mom and Dad's room, and I'm going to sleep in my own room. What are you going to wear at night? Do you have a toothbrush in your bag? Can we go have pizza for dinner?''

Kate smiled as she put a hand out and ruffled Cody's hair. The twin beacons of excitement blazing out of his eyes reminded her of Brady, the first time she'd seen him.

''Kate?'' Cody repeated, anxious for his plans to be confirmed.

''We'll have to go to my apartment and pick up a nightgown, my toothbrush and a change of clothes and, yes, we can stop off at the pizza place for dinner.''

Unable to control himself, Cody wrapped his arms around Kate's waist and hugged her. ''I love you, Kate.''

''I love you, too, Cody.''

If only everything else were as easy as making Cody happy.

Chapter Five

Kate felt something wriggle against her back. She came wide-awake with a start. Her startled gaze took in the walls of the Brighams' living room, and a moment later she realized Cody had gotten into bed with her.

"G'morning, Kate! Are you awake?"

Looking at her watch, Kate realized it was eight o'clock. "It's late," she announced, struggling to sit up.

She rarely overslept, but it had been past two before she'd been able to fall asleep in the strange bed.

"I know." Cody beamed at her. "Uncle Brady's making breakfast."

"He's here?" Kate dragged the quilt up to her chin as the sounds and smells from the kitchen began to register.

"He's making coffee. He said I could have some with lots of milk." Cody watched her carefully.

"That's fine," Kate agreed, her mind on Brady. When had he come in?

"Morning, sleepyhead!"

He came out of the kitchen with two steaming mugs of coffee, set them down on the end table and disappeared into the kitchen again. "I'm fixing your coffee, Cody. I'll be back in a minute."

Kate tugged the quilt higher. His suave appearance in blue slacks, gray shirt and silk tie made her feel like left-over meat loaf.

Returning to the room, Brady handed Cody a plastic glass with cartoon characters all over it. A glance showed Kate it was only half-filled, and therefore easy for Cody to manage.

"You didn't sleep upstairs."

The intense look that accompanied Brady's question made her insides quiver.

Kate shook her head. She had taken one look at the picture of Jack and Maura Brigham on the wall of their bedroom, and fled downstairs, feeling as if she were trespassing. In the picture, Cody's mother was leaning over her husband's back, her hands on his shoulders. Jack Brigham was laughing up at his wife, their love plain for all the world to see.

"This couch pulls out into a great bed," was the only explanation she offered.

"I know how great it is," Brady commented wryly. "I've slept on it before. You're going to be stiff today."

The recollection of how he'd massaged the stiffness out of her neck at the zoo made her feel hot all over. "I'll be fine," Kate said quickly. "How long have you been here?"

Brady raised one brow. "Cody let me in when I rang the bell half an hour ago."

"I asked who it was first, before I unlocked the door, jus' like you tole me to, Kate." Cody seemed worried about her reaction.

"You did good, Cody." Kate's gaze sped from the little boy back to Brady as the latter said, "I saw you asleep and decided to make some coffee. Don't you want it?"

"I like it to cool off, before I drink it." Actually, she didn't want to reach for it, and risk the quilt slipping.

Brady looked at her and then got to his feet. "Cody, how about going upstairs and getting dressed, while I start on your pancakes? That'll give Kate some time to get ready."

"I can fix breakfast," Kate said.

"It's no problem," replied Brady. "I've taken the rest of the day off."

Another day off? Kate's heart sank. Brady seemed perfectly content to remain a stranger to regular work.

As Cody raced up the stairs, Brady turned to her, "Don't feel bad about not waking up earlier. I know how hard it is to fall asleep on that bed."

What Brady didn't know was that the pull-out bed wasn't the only reason she hadn't fallen asleep quickly. The picture in his sister's room had ignited a deep ache of longing inside Kate, setting off the usual tug-of-war between her mind and her heart.

Maura was lucky to have found both love and security. After tossing and turning for hours, Kate had told herself Cody's parents were living proof that she had to be patient about finding Mr. Right, as well.

Brady stared at the eggs in the pan. He hadn't expected Kate to be asleep when he'd unlocked the front door. The flower softness of her face in repose, with one hand tucked under her cheek, had made him want to stand and stare. What would her reaction have been if he'd dropped to his knees and kissed her awake?

Instead of giving in to the urge, he'd walked into the kitchen, like a gentleman. Not that all this gentlemanly stuff was getting him anywhere, Brady thought gloomily. Both his luck and St. Patrick seemed to be ignoring him these days.

"Something's burning." Kate rushed in, just as the smoke alarm went off.

They both stared at the black mess in the frying pan.

"I wasn't paying attention," Brady said quickly.

"Did you burn my breakfast, Uncle Brady?" Cody asked anxiously, coming into the kitchen.

Above his head, the adults exchanged a laughing look. "It looks like I did, buddy. I'm sorry. There aren't any more eggs, so how about if I take you and Kate out for breakfast? After that we can go to the toy store and see if that part we ordered for your train set has come in."

Kate's smile faded. Spending time with Brady was dangerous to her self-control, but there was no way out of the situation. She'd been hired to watch Cody, so she'd have to go along.

The silence told her both Cody and his uncle were waiting for an answer. "I'll get my bag and join you."

Four hours later, Brady stared at the picture Kate and Cody made on the couch. Tired out from playing with his train set and the new caboose they had bought, Cody had climbed on the couch, snuggled against Kate's arm as she read him a story and promptly fallen asleep.

Kate settled Cody comfortably on the couch, fetching a sheet to cover him with, before sitting back down and opening one of her schoolbooks.

Brady stared at her. Right through breakfast, stopping off at the toy store, and assembling Cody's train set on the kitchen floor, she had maintained a keep-your-distance air of friendliness.

Now, watching her study, one would think he wasn't even in the same room with her. The barrier was definitely back in place.

"I better give you a check for this week before I forget."

Kate looked up in surprise. Maura had insisted on paying her a week's salary in advance before she left, and she had assumed she would be paid every two weeks from now on.

"How much do you charge for watching kids overnight?"

Kate stared at Brady. His pen was poised over his checkbook. "Nothing. Maura's paying me very generously as it is, and I was glad to help out in an emergency."

The wheels in Brady's brain turned furiously, and he couldn't help smiling as he wrote out a check.

Kate looked up from the check he had handed her, to catch the grin on his face. "What's so funny?" she asked suspiciously.

"Nothing."

You are, Brady wanted to shout. *You're no more mercenary than Santa Claus and good St. Patrick rolled into one. If you were, you wouldn't have refused the extra money I was offering you.*

Pleased, he returned to his magazine and actually managed to concentrate on the article he was reading.

Across from him, Kate lifted her head from time to time to stare at him, a puzzled frown on her face.

Sunday morning, Kate woke early, dressed and wandered around her apartment. Another nightmare had taken her back to her childhood, bringing back the feeling of tremendous fear and helplessness that had trapped her all her growing years. She had woken with a jolt, heart pounding, the smear of tears on her cheeks.

Standing by the window in a shaft of sunlight, she let the warmth dispel the last bit of lingering fear. Since her teens, she had contemplated every move in her life like a master chess player, engaging in weighty thought before every step. She had to use every advantage to end up a winner.

So far she'd done well. Kate's gaze brightened as she took in the airy brightness of her apartment. The Guthries were an easygoing couple in their forties, who generally spent five days out of a month at home. In the nine months Kate had lived here, they had become her friends.

All she had to do was keep an eye on the place, the gardener and the cleaning service. Once a week, she walked through the main house, to make sure everything was in order, watered the plants and reset the alarm.

The beautiful two-story house was part of an exclusive tract of custom homes in Jacaranda Meadows known as Goldrush Hill. Forty-five minutes away from downtown Los Angeles, the development gave one the impression of being far away from the noise and grime of the city.

Moving here was one of the best things she had done for herself. It hadn't taken long to find her present job in the preschool, next to the shopping center in Jacaranda Meadows. Resigning from her job as assistant manager in the large department store she had worked in since she had turned sixteen, severed Kate's final link with the past.

Every move took her further away from the physical reality of her past, but the darkness of her memories still returned to haunt her at night.

The college she'd transferred her credits to was just fifteen minutes away from Jacaranda Meadows. It would take another two years of part-time schooling to get her teaching degree, but Kate was happy with the way things were. To look at her now, no one would guess what a long way she had come already.

Financially, things looked good. The money she was making watching Cody would help pay next semester's tuition. She would even have a little left over. And there were so many preschools in the area, she shouldn't have trouble finding another job when the Brighams returned. Just to be sure, Kate had mailed her résumé to a dozen preschools she had found in the Yellow Pages.

Brady. Kate paused and took a deep breath. She wasn't sure if he was a blessing to count, or danger in disguise. True, he had gotten her this job, and was a wonderful person, except for his allergy to hard work. It was just that she didn't know how long she could withstand the effect he had on her. Her brain became mush when he was around. Even the lying she had taken up as if it were second nature to her, didn't help.

Harold. Kate bit her lip. He had called again last night, suggesting they go out for a drink. She had refused kindly, but firmly. From Harold's tone, she'd guessed he wouldn't be calling her again.

Where was the necessity to let Harold go in such a hurry? her brain demanded.

You can't keep someone dangling, when you're not interested in him. Harold's a nice guy, her heart insisted.

It isn't as if there is a lineup of rich, single men waiting to propose to you, her brain pointed out.

"I have to be in love with the man I marry."

Kate raised a hand to her mouth as if wishing the words back. She felt guilty—that criterion had only been added to her list of what she wanted in Mr. Right since she'd met Brady. It complicated everything.

No one knew better than Kate how hard she had struggled to get to where she was now. So far she deserved an A for achievement. Which was all the more reason to be very careful around Brady. She couldn't afford to throw everything she had worked for away on a whim.

The three staccato raps on the door startled Kate so much she spilled some of the tea from the mug she held. Luckily, her daydreaming had let it grow cold and she wasn't scalded.

Kate hurried to the door, and flung it open. The Guthries, concerned about her safety when they were away, had installed an additional security door with a deadbolt lock. The metal design of the outer door allowed her a clear glimpse of the man on her doorstep.

Being Brady, he *would* know where she lived, Kate thought in bemusement.

''Good morning!''

Unlocking the security door, she stared at him, amazed by the wave of gladness that surged up in her. The next instant, her thoughts flew to Cody. ''Is something wrong? Do your parents want me to watch Cody? Is your mother's cousin worse?''

He leaned against the door and said, ''Whoa! Let me catch my breath for a minute, will you? Cody's fine. So is Cousin Ellen.''

Kate's gaze shied away from those powerful eyes to slide down his body. The damp T-shirt and the navy jogging shorts emphasized the fact there was not a spare ounce of fat on Brady. Sweat flowed in tiny rivulets down his brow and the side of his face. He adjusted the strap to his backpack, but even that casual movement oozed sensuality.

"Aren't you going to ask me in?" The reminder held a gently teasing note.

He clearly needed a rest before he jogged back. With a frozen smile on her face, Kate stood aside and said, "Of course. Please come in."

Brady hobbled past her and sank into one of the chairs by the folding card table that served both as a study and eating area.

"Jogging is not for me," Brady panted, massaging his chest. "Definitely not for me."

Kate's eyes widened. Last week, the evening news had covered the story of a young man who'd had a fatal heart attack because he'd suddenly taken up jogging, without getting his doctor's approval.

"Brady, are you all right? Do you normally jog? Does your chest hurt? Should I . . . ?"

"I'm fine, just winded."

Kate wondered if he'd been teasing her. Her gaze shied away from his laughing, knowing eyes to follow a single trail of sweat down Brady's neck. Her hands longed to touch his slick shoulders, then follow through with her lips.

She turned away abruptly. So much for the mental reinforcement she indulged in every morning. Two minutes with Brady, and it melted. Fetching a towel from the linen closet opposite her bathroom, Kate handed it to Brady.

"Thanks." Brady mopped his face, put the towel down and massaged his chest again.

Kate felt worry mushroom inside her. "Brady, why do you keep rubbing your chest?"

"Oh, that—" Brady dropped his hand "—I walked into an open cupboard yesterday, and the edge caught me there. I've got a real beauty of a bruise. Want to see?"

Kate moved back and said sharply, "No. Of course not."

Brady grinned at her tone. "Pity. Thought you might offer to kiss it and make it all better, like you do with Cody."

Kate's face burned, but Brady wasn't looking at her. His gaze lingered on the hem of her old blue shorts, transmitting smiling appreciation as their eyes met again. Kate bit her lower lip and smiled uncertainly as a gush of nervousness swamped her entire system. Her bones felt as if they were melting under the heat of his look. She wanted to yell at Brady to stop eyeing her as if she were his favorite flavor of ice cream, but the words wouldn't come out.

Give yourself a ten for eloquence every time he's around, woman.

"Would you like some tea or coffee? A cold drink?" Kate looked at the open book on the card table. Maybe he'd get the message she was busy and leave.

Brady seemed in no hurry to answer.

"Tea, please," Brady finally said and Kate moved away, glad to be able to turn her back on him.

Hadn't anyone told the man knees weren't edible?

She waited for the water to boil, fussing around with the mugs and tea bags—anything, to avoid turning back to him. As the kitchen was simply an alcove off her living-cum-dining area, she knew Brady watched her every move.

She should have put on something else this morning, but she hadn't been expecting company.

"How long have you lived here?"

"Almost a year." Kate took out a bag of sugar and filled a container with some.

Brady had taken in every detail of Kate's apartment. The living area held a couch, a small end table and a thirteen-inch television set on a stand. The card table had a chair on either side. Against one wall was a metal filing cabinet that had obviously seen better days.

The whole place was spotlessly clean, but something about it bothered him. There was nothing in this room that betokened the warmth and love Katie was capable of. Not a single cushion, picture or personal knick-knack. Suddenly he had to know more about Katie.

"Did you know the Guthries before you moved here?"

"No, I just saw their ad in the paper and I applied for the job. One of my teachers gave me an excellent reference, and they decided to hire me on the spot."

Her clipped answer made it obvious she wasn't going to tell him any more. Brady frowned. It was as if Katie didn't want anyone to see beyond the tough facade she chose to present to the world. As if she were scared to let go of the tight hold she had over herself even here and express her true personality.

She wasn't tough and she wasn't cold. One only had to watch her with Cody to see how much love she had to share. She played with him, caring for him as if she really loved the four-year-old. Brady had never seen her impatient with Cody's endless chatter, or too tired to play a new game with him.

Her stubbornness could get Brady as mad as a disturbed hornet, but when he reviewed everything they'd said and done, and remembered the way Katie had melted against him when he'd kissed her at the zoo, he knew there was nothing wrong with his first impression. Katie was all woman. His.

It was just a matter of time before she realized that fact.

Didn't believe in love, was it? The lawyer in him was going to enjoy proving her wrong. And the man in him was going to be waiting for her when she came out of the cold monolith of reason she had entombed herself in, and tumbled into his arms.

Kate cleared her throat, and Brady guessed the silence was making her nervous.

"Been studying?" he asked, glancing at the open book.

"Yes."

It was strange Katie hadn't asked him why he was here. Removing the backpack from his shoulders, Brady extracted the book that had given him an excuse for coming over. "I brought one of your textbooks back. Cody thought you might need it to study."

He didn't mention the single sheet of paper that had slipped out of the book. Written down on it was an account of every penny Katie had spent in the past two weeks.

Kate looked at the book in Brady's hand. No wonder he was out of breath if he had jogged the three miles from his parents' home to Goldrush Hill with a heavy book weighing him down. She supposed this was no time to tell him she had left the book at the condominium because she didn't need it till Monday.

"Thank you."

As she carried the tea mugs to the card table, she saw the small gift-wrapped package on it.

"What's that?"

"Happy Birthday, Kate!" He held out the elegant green-and-silver foil wrapped box.

Kate set the mugs down so hard, she spilled some of the tea. Grabbing a couple of napkins from the holder on the table, she mopped up the mess.

"How do you know?" she asked blankly.

"It's on your driver's license."

"Oh!"

Kate's mind went back to Bernie's Gifts and Luggage. Brady had asked her for identification to verify her check, and she'd handed him her driver's license. He had barely seemed to glance at it, but apparently he had a great memory.

"Do you have something special planned for today?"

"No."

Kate sank into the chair across from Brady. She never celebrated her birthday. Picking up her mug, she buried her face in it.

"Aren't you going to open your present, Kate?" His warm velvety voice slid down her spine, flicking her nerve endings like a whip, and she jumped. Her knees felt like modeling clay as she reached for the package.

Kate opened the four-inch square box with fingers that shook.

"Thank you." She stared at the wild violets in the glass paperweight as if her life depended on keeping them in sight. Somehow, it didn't surprise her that Brady remembered how much she'd liked it.

It was strange the way Brady could, effortlessly, get closer to her than anyone ever had in her entire life. She didn't like the feeling. Letting someone into the secret regions of one's heart and soul meant vulnerability. And the high-wire act Brady was trying to tempt her with, could only end in disaster for her.

"Many happy returns, Katie." Brady covered one of her hands with his own. His touch sent heat hurtling through her central nervous system, till every nerve end-ing quivered.

Slipping her hand out from under his, Kate picked up her mug, and took a huge gulp of tea. Brady had done it again. Encroached on the tight wall of self control she had maintained so effortlessly in the past and toppled it, brick by weightless brick. Only Mama and Rose had ever called her Katie. Strangely enough, hearing the name on Brady's lips didn't bother her.

Brady watched her cautiously. He wanted to have her in his arms, tell her he loved her and ask her to marry him. He wanted to yell his new-found knowledge to the world…"Brady loves Katie!" Then he wanted to take her out and buy her emeralds for her birthday, to match her eyes. Yesterday he had almost given in to the urge to get a heart-shaped pendant, set with tiny glowing emeralds and diamonds, but with Katie that just might be the fi-nal straw as far as he was concerned.

Doing what he wanted, had been plan A.

Used to women who recognized their feelings and de-manded fulfillment as easily as a child asked for candy, this continuous war of self-denial Katie waged with her-self baffled Brady. In his circle, kisses were given as ca-sually as smiles. With Katie, he'd felt like a trespasser the first time they'd kissed, till she'd responded to him.

At times he felt like telling her what he really did for a living, that he was better off than two Harolds put to-gether, but pride always held him back. For both their sakes, he wanted to be certain it was love that melded them together.

It wouldn't be hard to sweep Katie off her feet and into bed with him, but he couldn't risk losing her. Not if he wanted forever with her, which he did. No, he'd have to exercise all the caution of a tightrope walker, the skill of a surgeon and the patience he didn't have, to win her.

It was time to try out plan B.

"Katie, will you spend the day with me?"

She looked up, startled, not quite sure what he wanted, stiffening as her heightened senses guessed at the palpable danger in his suggestion.

"I have to study."

The words came out weakly. She ought to have said Harold was taking her out, anything that would put distance between them, but she couldn't.

Though she felt like a child atop a wobbling stool, reaching for a forbidden treat, Kate knew she couldn't stop herself from accepting Brady's invitation if he insisted. Twenty-four years was too long to have gone without celebrating a birthday.

Brady rushed on before the uncertainty he glimpsed in her eyes hardened into refusal. He didn't even want to entertain the thought that Harold might be taking her out. "A friend's lent me his boat for the day. I'll bring a picnic and we can anchor in this cove I know, relax and swim. It's such a nice day, I'm sure the water will be warm enough to swim in."

If for some reason the water *wasn't* warm enough, thought Kate, it would heat up by the time she'd been in it awhile. She was generating enough steam to operate a power plant.

"Katie?" Brady's voice prodded, gently reminding her he was still waiting for an answer.

"I could get some shells and sand for a craft project with Cody," Kate said aloud, as if trying to justify accepting the invitation to herself.

"Sure," said Brady easily.

He'd get the whole beach for her, if only she would agree to spend the day with him.

Everyone has a right to celebrate at least one birthday in their lives, Kate's heart argued.

Spending time with Brady isn't going to help your willpower any, warned her brain.

"I don't know a thing about boats," Kate said hesitantly. "I've never been on one. I might get seasick."

What she really wanted to say was, "I might fall in love with you, Brady, and then what would I do?"

Cupping her hands around her mug, she willed the warmth to reach into her shivering confusion and still it.

"There's only one way of finding out, isn't there?" Brady reasoned. "I've got patches for motion sickness that you can wear behind your ear, or you can take a tablet. And if you really don't like being on the boat, we can always come back. Look, you can even take your book and study if you want to, while you lie on deck and get a tan."

Reluctantly Kate met his eyes and felt herself being caught up and swept along by swirling, debilitating, polar currents again. In spite of the hint of danger being alone with Brady for an entire day entailed, it would be better than sitting here with her thoughts.

She didn't answer Brady for so long, that he swore he could taste the sharp edge of her refusal. Her green eyes watching him over the rim of her mug, reminded him of those of a rabbit trapped in a corner, wondering, terrified, what to do next. And that hurt.

"For just one day, can't you forget everything?" What was it about her that made pleading worthwhile? "Can't we just be a man and a woman spending a day together?" A flush tinted Kate's cheeks, and Brady said, "No, scratch that man and woman bit. Make it friends spending the day together. Surely there's nothing wrong with that?''

Of course, not, agreed her heart.

Yes, there is, reminded Kate's brain, *if the man is Brady.*

"I'll come." The words rushed out of her, as if in a hurry to get away from the sternness of rational thinking.

"You will?" For a minute Brady looked so surprised, Kate almost laughed aloud. He recovered quickly, though. "Great. I'll pick you up in an hour. Don't change. Those blue shorts are perfect. Bring a swimsuit, too."

"I'll pack the picnic," Kate began, only to be interrupted.

"No, don't do that. My mother has plenty of food in the refrigerator." Brady crossed his fingers behind his back. "I've got everything under control. I'll be back in an hour."

"Would you like me to give you a ride back?" Kate asked, remembering the condition he'd arrived in.

"No, thanks." Brady smiled at her. "I need the exercise."

Her spirits bubbling with anticipation, Kate showered and got ready for the day as soon as Brady left.

She put on a black maillot that had three contrasting bands of color at the waist—green, white and, her favorite, aqua. Slipping into jeans, she reached into her closet for a white, crocheted cover-up that reached to midthigh.

Packing a change of clothing, a toiletry bag and a towel into a large straw bag took only a few more minutes. At the last minute, Kate added one of her books. It made her feel just slightly less guilty about the day.

The tight smile Kate gave him when he returned to pick her up told Brady she was having second thoughts about going out with him. Picking up the dark glasses he had removed to say hello, he jammed them on his nose. He had to give her time. The fact she'd agreed to go with him was such a big break, he'd felt as if he had a four-leaf clover in his pocket.

Not wanting to remind Kate about Harold, Brady hadn't mentioned the man. He intended filling Kate's life with so much love, she'd have a hard time even remembering the man's name.

Brought up to believe he could do anything he set his mind to, Brady's first thought had been that persuading Katie to declare her love for him was just a matter of time. Now his self-confidence had taken a nosedive. Even the perennially optimistic, Irish part of him admitted winning Katie wouldn't be easy.

Far from wanting to give up, Brady looked forward to the challenges that lay ahead. That included not just carrying on an active campaign to tear down her inhibitions, but getting Kate to change her views on love. As a replacement for a wall made of stone and mortar that shut out emotion and dealt only in cold hard facts, love held no equal. His parents, and his sister, were living proof of that.

Chapter Six

The custom-built cruiser was much bigger and very different from anything Kate had imagined. Its green and white paint looked spanking new, and the reflection from the trim dazzled the eye.

Brady showed her around after they boarded the boat and then left her in the cabin, telling her to join him on the bridge when she was ready.

As soon as he'd gone, Kate peeped into the forward stateroom again. The first time she'd seen the queen-size bed with its inviting cushions, her heart had stopped. Spending the day with him had suddenly seemed very complicated. Brady, however, had simply reached over her shoulder and closed the sliding door, shutting the area from view, amputating her fears.

The cockpit area, an ultramodern galley with a dinette opposite—that converted into another bed and another aft sleeping area—shared space with a bathroom that had a walk-in shower, vanity and mirror. The dream boat could compete with a five-star hotel for luxury accommodations. Didn't borrowing something this expensive make Brady very nervous?

Kate stared at her reflection in the mirror after she'd slipped off her jeans and top. Her glowing eyes wore the expression of a stranger, ready for any adventure.

Kate hesitantly climbed the ladder to the bridge. The marina was quickly becoming a speck in the distance.

Brady had removed his bright Hawaiian shirt and white cutoffs, and was at the wheel in black swimming trunks, a life jacket and a pair of sunglasses. The bronzed muscles of his back and legs reminded her of a Greek statue. The bare expanses of his skin invited her touch.

For a moment, Kate was tempted to bolt down the stainless steel-ladder and remain in the cabin for the rest of the day.

She forced herself to go stand beside him, her eyes sweeping over the instrument panel.

"Hi!" Kate said shyly.

Brady turned and she felt his gaze taking in every inch of her inside and outside the black maillot.

"Hi! How are you feeling?"

Kate had forgotten all about being seasick. Obviously the tablet she'd taken as a precaution was working well. "I'm fine."

The surprise in her voice made Brady throw his head back and laugh. The roar of sound, so typically Brady, made Kate's pulses leap.

"You'd forgotten all about it," he said, chuckling. "That's good. Put on some suntan lotion and a life jacket, and then you can sunbathe up here, or relax in the cabin. I'm going to take the *Shenondoah* out to my favorite place, and then we can swim."

"*Shenondoah?* Is that what this boat is called?" Kate asked as she got into a life jacket.

"Uh-huh."

He turned to face her and Kate's eyes were drawn to his chest. A smattering of dark hair was all she could see between the two vertical bands of the life jacket he wore.

"I never mind being looked over by a beautiful woman. It's important that we men put our wares in the window these days. How else can we attract anyone?"

The teasing words and Brady's highly suggestive remark made Kate's face burn, and she said quickly, "Who owns this boat?"

With his eyes hidden behind the glasses, Kate couldn't judge Brady's expression, but his tone changed as he said slowly, "She's owned by a family actually. Three people have shares in her."

"She's beautiful."

Kate lifted her face, enjoying the sun and breeze on her face. Brady watched as she stood a little away from him, feet braced slightly to accommodate the boat's motion, hands hanging down at her side, eyes closed. Her hair was in its usual coronet, drawing attention to the long slender neck. The curve of her body in the modest swimsuit, which looked like something his grandmother would have liked to wear, had Brady's hands clenching the steering wheel.

It wasn't hard to imagine Katie in an itsy-bitsy bikini. Green. A green one with white dots.

"Want to steer her?" Brady offered as she turned to look at him.

"May I?"

The eager look on her face reminded him of Cody as he said, "Sure. There's nothing to it."

Hesitantly Kate got behind the wheel and placed her hands on it. Brady stood beside her, keeping one hand on the wheel while he explained the mechanics of controlling a fully powered cruiser. He could have used the moment as an excuse to come up behind her and hold the steering wheel with both hands, imprisoning her in the cradle of his arms, but he chose not to. He had given her his word he would treat her as just a friend today, and he meant to keep it.

Gradually Kate relaxed, lulled by the way the boat purred along and by the heady power that she was actually controlling it herself, if Brady was to be believed. Carefully she listened while he explained boating rules and regulations, and how to call for help on the radio if an emergency occurred.

The wind and excitement whipped up the color in her cheeks, and she could feel her body soaking up the sun. Kate hadn't felt this good in a long time.

"Brady!"

A sudden look around showed him nowhere close, and she panicked.

"What is it, Katie?" He came up the steps, with two cans of soda in his hands.

"Don't leave me," Kate begged. What if she steered wrong, or capsized the expensive boat?

"Never, Kate." He came to stand beside her. "Want a drink?"

"Please."

He handed her a can, watching as she tipped her head back and took a long, deep swallow.

"Thanks." Like an anxious driver, her eyes didn't shift from the horizon.

"Relax, Kate. There's a lot of water out here, and I don't see anyone else in the passing lane."

"I'll try," Kate said, laughing.

As Brady said, there was a great deal of ocean out here. Besides, he wouldn't let her make any wrong moves.

Kate stared at the water, almost blinded by the fact that had just surfaced. There was no denying it. She felt safe with Brady, trusted him not to let her down. Trust was not something she had experienced with a man before.

Brady took over after half an hour, veering to the east slightly. "We'll be there in ten minutes."

A glance at her watch showed Kate it was eleven o'clock. They'd been on the water for an hour and a half.

When Brady anchored in a secluded cove, Kate was surprised all over again. The place was like a movie set. In the distance she could see a small beach. The cliffs behind it towered over them, like gigantic columns from another age. Above, the sky was so blue, it almost hurt to look at it. There was no other sign of human habitation, no sound other than the gentle *lap-lap* of water against the side of the boat, the call of a lonely gull. The scents of the ocean mixed with the spicy tang of Brady's cologne. Kate licked the salty spray from her lips and took a deep breath.

"This place is gorgeous. Where are we?"

"Brady's Cove," he said solemnly. "I own exclusive rights, but I'm willing to share with you. I'll have the deeds drawn up Monday to make it legal."

Kate laughed and Brady's gaze dropped to her mouth as he said, "Another day when we have more time, we'll have a picnic on the beach."

He'd deliberately dropped anchor a good distance away from the pier. Time wasn't the only reason he didn't want to go to the arc of soft sand today. Brady didn't know if he could resist making love to Kate once he took her there. Set back on the cliffs, so it wasn't visible from here, was the vacation home his parents had bought several years ago. And taking Katie there was one temptation he didn't want to risk.

"Shall we swim now?"

She nodded and he stepped onto the swim platform, helping her onto it, before he dived into the water. Kate dived in after Brady, reveling at the icy cold water against her heated flesh. Coming up, she struck out strongly, aware, by the churning of the water, that Brady was right beside her.

They swam for half an hour before returning to the boat. That he meant to keep his word about them spending the day as friends became very evident with each passing hour. Not once, by look, gesture or word did he do anything to give her any cause for alarm.

Which, Kate told herself fiercely, was what she wanted after all. So why wasn't she happy about it?

"You swim well." Brady's voice was muffled by the towel he was using to absorb the water from his hair. He spread the towel out on the deck, the ripple of muscles under his skin creating waves of longing in Kate.

"Thanks." All the lessons she'd taken had been part of her plan to find Mr. Right. Grooming herself so she could be Mrs. Right, had taken willpower and discipline.

Brady patted the surface of the towel he had laid out for her, a narrow three inches of deck demarcating it from his. Kate sank down on it, wishing life came with a sophisticated control panel, as well.

Protected by the canvas cover over the bridge, they napped without fear of waking up broiled. When she awoke, Kate turned her head to look at Brady. He appeared touchingly vulnerable in sleep. Her hand came up, and before she could stop herself, one finger traced the outline of his mouth.

His eyes flew open and she saw the blaze that swept through them as he realized what she was doing. Snatching back the finger that seemed glued to the corner of his mouth, Kate sat up and reached for the suntan lotion again.

What on earth was the matter with her? Brady would think she was some sort of a tease, deliberately blowing hot and cold.

Brady lifted one of his brows. To say she had taken him by surprise, was putting it mildly. He was elated, because it was the first time Kate had touched him voluntarily. There was definitely a four-leaf clover in his pocket.

A movement behind her a few minutes later, told Kate Brady had sat up, as well.

"This is the life," she heard him say, his voice still slightly sleep-roughened and very sexy. "Sometimes I think I'd like to sail around the world in a boat. Days on end with nothing except the sun, the ocean and one's thoughts for company."

Kate's excitement dwindled. Brady was a dreamer. And Mama had always called Chuck Langdon a dangerous dreamer, because he had never stopped dreaming. Did Brady know there was a time for dreaming and a time for working? A time for working hard to put foundations under one's castles in the air and turn them into reality? While winners did the latter, losers just kept dreaming.

"It would be nice, if one could afford it," Kate said, "but it would take a great deal of planning and saving."

On a salesman's salary, it would also take a miracle.

"Have you ever done something just because you
wanted to?" Some of the impatience he felt came
through clearly in his voice.

"No," said Kate, "I can't afford impulses."

The way her face changed warned him he was getting
in too deep again.

"Hungry?" Brady asked quickly, in an effort to
change the subject.

"Starving," Kate said, not clear if it was food she was
hungry for.

Brady insisted she sit at the dinette while he unpacked
the huge cooler he had carried aboard.

They feasted on crackers, caviar, cold cracked crab and
an assortment of hors d'oeuvres and salads followed by
some of the largest, juiciest strawberries Kate had ever
seen. His mother must have the best-stocked refrigerator
in the country, she thought, to be able to produce fresh
strawberries in January.

Egged on by Brady, Kate sampled everything, relish-
ing the adventures her taste buds were having. Brady even
produced a can of whipped cream for the strawberries,
but Kate preferred to eat them as they were, reveling in
the slight edge of tartness some of them had.

"That's the best meal I've ever had." Replete, she
leaned back and stretched her legs out in front of her.

The banquette they sat at in the cabin below deck was
a soft pearly gray. White curtains with a pink-and-gray
ribboned border gently fluttered behind them, comple-
menting the gray carpet. Above them what looked like
the sunroof in a car was open, letting in light and a gentle breeze.

That Brady used the boat often was obvious by the way
he handled it. She was sure he didn't take it out alone.
Kate wondered what his other companions were like.

Pretty, sexy and liberated? Did they make good use of the sleeping accommodations?

"Wake up, sleepyhead." Brady's gentle teasing brought her back. "I'll teach you how to play gin rummy."

They played cards, listened to some music on the little radio, and then later they swam again. It was definitely cooler when they got out of the water the second time, and Brady said, "We'll have to head for home soon."

He showered first while Kate lingered on deck. She didn't want this day to end. Eyes dreamy, she stared across the water, imagining a little cottage in the cove, a man and a woman who loved each other, their children.

With your dimples and Brady's eyes?

A shudder not entirely due to the cooling temperature went through her. Her heart was running amok. Brady had been a perfect gentleman. Not by word or gesture had he done anything to create any kind of sexual awareness. In fact, the very care he had taken not to initiate or prolong even the simplest physical contact had driven her crazy. She was about to go out of her mind with longing. Kate wanted nothing more than to throw herself into his arms and twine her fingers through his black hair, and beg him to bring her fantasies to life.

Weakness flooded Kate. She'd never reacted to any other man like this. The hormones she'd always been convinced were *under*active had gone from dormant to alive to frenetic too quickly.

Sometime later, Kate showered and came out to see Brady seated at the dinette, a huge cake in front of him. Her gaze fixed on the three candles he'd put in the center, and she couldn't move.

He lit the candles and sang "Happy Birthday" to her, before he noticed the tears in her eyes.

"What's wrong?" he asked, getting to his feet and coming to stand beside her.

"N-nothing." A single tear trailed down her cheek, and Kate lifted a finger to blot it away.

"Blow the candles out, unless you like wax in your chocolate frosting," Brady said.

She smiled, and bent to blow the candles out.

"Why three?" she asked.

"For health, wealth and happiness. I hope you'll always be happy, Katie."

"Thank you, Brady."

"Did you make a wish?"

Startled, Kate shook her head.

"Come on, woman. One would think you'd never had a cake before."

Kate froze, willing herself to shut out the pain Brady's words inflicted. The things she'd never had, he took for granted.

Her tense face warned Brady he'd stepped on her toes in some way.

"You're only allowed one wish, not a hundred." He hoped the joke would bring her out of her mood.

Katie smiled, but Brady didn't miss the strained look in her eyes. He watched in silence as she forced herself to swallow some of the cake and then excused herself and went up on deck.

Whatever had happened in the past few minutes had taken him back to square one. Going over everything, much as he would a defense he was preparing, yielded no clues. Maybe Katie just wasn't into cakes, or they triggered memories of an unhappy birthday. Or something.

So much, thought Brady, for plan B. He'd have to come up with a plan C—fast.

Kate watched the sky. The vibrancy of the sunset was a perfect match for the pell-mell confusion of her thoughts. Her watercolor life had suddenly taken on all the bright hues in front of her. It was as if a master artist had decided to repaint the canvas of her life in vivid oils. Demanding, uncontrollable, *dangerous*.

Brady occupied a major portion of the canvas. Too much for her peace of mind.

Their upbringings were so different, they had very little in common. She had better get back on track. She had to forget Brady, and continue her search for Mr. Right. As she stared at the changing sky, Kate admitted to herself that she had never felt less enthusiastic about anything in her life.

Brady came up on deck and handed her a sweatshirt. "It's getting cold."

"It's been a beautiful day. Thank you for asking me to share it with you, Brady." The forced note of cheerfulness in Kate's voice told him she was back behind the barrier she never left home without.

"It's not over yet." He startled her by putting a finger on her lips. "When we get back I want you to have dinner with me at this seafood shanty. It's really old and not very chic, but the food is out of this world."

Made powerless by the heat pouring through her veins at the touch of his finger on her mouth, Kate could only nod. The scent of Brady lingered in the sweatshirt he'd given her. It wrapped her in warmth, befuddling her mind. Having dinner with him seemed a wonderful idea.

Tomorrow, she'd go back to her original plan.

Kate wasn't surprised when her doorbell rang the next morning at nine. She invited Brady in, her gaze registering his gray slacks and burgundy silk shirt. Most of last night had been spent telling herself it was risky to let what was between her and Brady go any further. It was becoming harder to remember her blueprint. With him she forgot what had happened to Mama and Rose. She couldn't afford to do that.

What she had planned to say to him would be easier said on the telephone, but now that he was here, she'd just get it over with.

"Not jogging today?"

"On the Sabbath?" His mock indignation made her laugh.

"Want some tea?"

Brady nodded. Had Katie expected him to come over? He'd mulled over everything last night. Yesterday had been wonderful. Katie hadn't mentioned money once. He wanted to suggest a drive out to the mountains today. The more time he could spend with her, the quicker he could convince her how important love was.

"Thank you for yesterday." Kate managed a smile in spite of the fact that Brady's eyes were kicking up a storm inside her. Dinner last night had been just as wonderful as Brady had promised. The small shanty had served the most delicious seafood she had ever eaten. "I didn't mean to fall asleep on the way home."

"It doesn't matter. You were tired." It had felt good to hear Katie's sleepy mumbled thanks as he'd stopped the car, know that she'd enjoyed the day.

She brought the tea-filled mugs to the card table, and sat down.

"You love the sea, don't you?" The way Brady had stood at the helm yesterday, the sight of him, at one with the sky and the ocean, would stay with her forever.

Brady nodded, wondering why Katie seemed so tense. Inwardly *he* tensed. The fact that she wasn't looking directly at him was a definite sign that something was amiss.

Kate took a deep breath. "Don't you wish you earned enough to buy your own boat?"

Brady put his mug down. "What do you mean?"

The quietly controlled yet puzzled quality of Brady's voice made her hesitate, but she couldn't back out of what had to be said. "You're smart enough to do anything. Why did you choose to work in a small store?"

"Maybe I like the laid-back life-style."

"You can do so much more," Kate persisted.

A demon of contrariness took hold of Brady. "Why should I?"

Kate held his gaze, though she felt her mouth tremble. "It's called working to full potential."

"Stop it." The cold incisiveness of his voice flooded her face with color, but she stuck to her guns.

"Yesterday you said we were friends, Brady," she reminded him. "I can't stand to see you throw your life away when there's so much you can do."

Brady's eyes darkened to the color of polished onyx. "Friends accept you for what you are."

"Friends," Kate flung at him, "tell you the truth about yourself."

"The truth being I should mold myself into your preconceived idea of what a man should be like, so that some woman can marry me for my money? Thanks, but no thanks."

"Financial security is an important factor in anyone's life."

"For someone like Harold maybe. My love will be all the security a woman needs." Placing a hand on the table, Brady leaned close to Kate. "With a little planning, a woman can achieve her *own* security, but no amount of money can buy her love.''

''Love grows where there's security,'' Kate persisted.

''You've locked yourself in a room without windows, haven't you, Katie? Your tunnel vision won't let you try love. You may not know it, but without love, you'll be poorer than you've ever been in your life. You're entitled to your views, but just don't ever treat me to a sermon like this again.''

Katie flinched, and Brady stared at her. He'd raised his voice, but Katie looked as if she expected him to strike her. Frustrated, he turned on his heel, walking over to the window.

Brady's anger brought back the old rhythm of fear, and Katie suddenly found it difficult to breathe. Her mind had lifted the curtain that she tried to keep drawn over the past and she had slipped back into the old abyss of pain. Her father had always shouted when he didn't get what he'd wanted, following it up with blows. Was physical domination every man's way of wielding power? Kate wrapped her arms around herself.

''D-don't you d-dare yell at m-me, Brady Gallagher.''

Kate couldn't believe she'd spoken. Mama had always said talking to an angry man was like fanning a flame. She tensed as Brady swung around to face her.

''I didn't mean to yell, but you have no business lecturing me on my life-style.'' Searching her pale features, Brady found he couldn't bear the look on Katie's face. He wasn't a two-headed monster, about to belch flame. Yet her shaking voice, and her trembling lips labeled him a bully. God, he had to get out of here, before he pulled her into his arms and made her tell him what was wrong. He smiled grimly. That would really endear him to her. ''I'd better leave now.''

Kate stared at the front door as it closed behind Brady, dumbfounded. It had all been her fault and *he'd* apologized? What was more, she'd found courage she didn't know she had, to stand up for herself. And Brady hadn't become angrier; he'd calmed down. What had just happened proved he wasn't anything like Chuck Langdon. What had just happened had also proved that Kate wasn't a replica of Mama and Rose. Could Mama have been wrong about all men being tarred with the same brush, about a woman's only recourse being to take whatever her man handed out?

Kate's mind went over what she'd said to Brady. Personal discoveries aside, what on earth had gotten into her? Brady was right. She had no business lecturing him about his life-style. Was she idiotic enough to want to try and turn him into Mr. Right?

No one knew better than her that it wasn't possible to change someone. Her father had been living proof of that. Why on earth had she thought Brady might listen to what she had to say?

Brady belonged in a world where people who weren't born with a silver spoon in their mouths simply bought them by the dozen. A world as far from the one she'd grown up in, as the earth was from sky. He would never believe that his circumstances might change, that it was important he depended only on himself, not his parents.

Brady's not the least bit like your father, so stop comparing them, her heart pointed out. *Chuck Langdon never apologized to anyone in his entire life.*

Doesn't change the fact he's still the playboy type, maintained her brain. *How's he going to support you unless he makes his own money? His parents aren't going to be thrilled about where you're from. You know they're classy people. They could cut him off without a penny, if he says he's marrying you. Think the love he talks of will stand a chance then?*

Kate wouldn't, *couldn't* put it to the test. The lessons of the past had been learned at too great a price for that.

Back at his parents' place, Brady changed his clothes before going into the garage. He and his father had picked up some wood from the lumberyard. They planned to convert the fourth garage into a playroom for Cody, and this seemed as good a time as any to start on the project. Picking up a two-by-four, Brady looked around for the tool belt and the hammer.

He hadn't been so smash-something furious in a long while. He was angry with Katie for clinging to her notions, and angry with himself because he just couldn't let go of her. Four weeks, and he hadn't made a dent in her way of thinking.

Pounding a nail in, he muttered a saying that had been his grandfather's favorite. "There's none so blind as those that won't see."

Why couldn't he accept the fact that Katie would never change, no matter what he did? Yesterday he'd practically had to sit on his hands not to reach out for a touch of that sensational skin, or use the pretext of helping her with the suntan lotion to feel the smooth nubile muscles of her back. And while he'd been trying to get her to trust him, she'd been wishing he made more money.

The worst part was, he didn't understand why it was so important to her to marry a rich man. Her needs were few and simple, she wasn't greedy. Could she have a secret ambition to become a society figure, or did she want the power that accompanied being rich?

The memory of her staring at him, as if he'd hit her—or would—gnawed at Brady. No matter what she'd said, he shouldn't have yelled at her. The truth was, he was angry at himself, as well. He was fed up with keeping up the pretense of being a salesman, tired of answering Katie's weekday inquiry about how things were at the store. Burned by the women who'd chased him for his money, wanting nothing more than to be loved for himself, he'd lied to Katie and made a mess of everything.

Upset as he was by her reasoning, he knew there had to be cause for Katie to be so set on marrying a man who could provide her with financial security. As a lawyer, he was trained to dig deep below the surface for his facts. He never held anyone guilty till he'd gathered hard, concrete facts that proved them so. Katie had told him she was poor, but there was more to this fixation of hers than that. There *had* to be. Pete Shroff's parents had been poor, but the man spent money as if it were water.

"Entered a nail-driving contest, son?"

Brady looked up at his father and then down at the two-by-four in front of him. The piece of wood had twelve nails hammered in, exactly two inches apart. "Just thinking, Dad."

"Must be quite a problem." His father had changed from his church suit into an old pair of jeans and a sweatshirt. Brady could hear his mother and Cody talking in the house.

"It is." Most people's problems didn't have a smile that haunted them night and day, and eyes that drove a man crazy with need. It didn't matter what Katie thought, or said, or did. He couldn't stop thinking about her, he couldn't stop loving her.

Something told Brady the four-leaf clover he'd imagined he'd had in his pocket yesterday was really a weed. His luck had vanished.

Chapter Seven

Kate huddled in bed, trying to think of dear familiar things. Nothing came to mind. She sneezed another five times, and then groaned.

"I'm never sick," she said defiantly.

Her stuffy nose weakened the effect of her words. She'd suddenly started sneezing Monday evening, and by the time she had returned from class, she'd developed a full-blown cold. She'd called Mrs. Gallagher, concerned about exposing Cody to her germs, and been told not to worry. Berry Gallagher and her husband had been thinking of taking Cody to their beach house, and this was as good a time as any. They planned to stay there for four days, so Kate was not to worry about a thing, except getting better.

Telling herself she'd be fine by this morning hadn't worked. The virus she had picked up seemed to be caused by tough germs immune to the power of positive thinking. Kate had stayed in bed all day, but she felt worse instead of better.

Misery clouded her mind as she wiped and blew her nose through another sneezing fit. When it was done, Kate lay back on her pillows and closed her eyes. In five minutes she'd get up, dress and go for a walk. Exercise was the answer....

The banging brought her wide-awake. Getting out of bed, Kate stumbled to the door and opened it, in the throes of the next fit of sneezing.

"Go away, Brady, I'm sick." Kate slammed her door shut.

The banging on the door started again, except this time it was followed by shouting. "Katie, open this door immediately. If you don't..."

But she did, not wanting the noise to bother the Guthries, who were home for a week. Though her apartment was over the garage and away from the main house, the couple spent a great deal of time in their garden in the evening. Kate didn't want them coming over to ask if anything was wrong. And that, she told herself, was the only reason she let Brady in. Really it was.

"Brady, what are you doing here?" she demanded as he shut the door behind himself. "You don't even like me anymore." Maybe he hadn't heard her the first time, she thought wearily.

"I never stopped liking you, Katie. I was just angry over some of the things you said, and I had to discuss what was bothering me. I didn't mean to yell at you, though."

She shouldn't have blown her nose so hard. It had to be the ringing in her ears that made her imagine the old warmth was back in his voice. "You don't need to catch my cold. Please go."

An extraloud sneeze at the end robbed the sentence of the authority she'd tried to speak with.

Brady had seen enough. Whisking her up in his arms, he carried her back to bed. All her protests didn't make a bit of difference.

"Where does it hurt, Katie? Have you seen a doctor?"

To hear his casual question, no one would guess the mercurylike fear coursing through his veins, pulling at his limbs with its leaden weight. Katie's body had been burning hot in his arms. When he'd brushed the hair off her forehead, it had been damp and sticky.

"Why are you here?"

"I'm here because whether you like it or not, I care about you."

The last shred of his anger had vanished the minute he'd heard she wasn't well. Seeing her had been all that mattered. "I'm not angry with you, Katie," he stressed. "We'll talk about it later."

"I'm sorry. I had no business saying the things I did, Brady."

The way her hand went up to rub her head told Brady it wasn't only the cold bothering her. Everything else faded before the fact that she was ill.

"Katie, have you taken any medicine for the fever?"

"Don't have a fever." Kate drew the quilt up to her chin, and wished she'd slipped into her flannel pajamas. Chills shook her body.

He stood up and reached for her.

"What are you doing?" asked Kate, feeling his hand go under her knees again.

"I'm taking you to Dr. Peters. He's our family doctor and he's very good."

"At this time of night?"

The words halted him. The Peters' and the Gallaghers' friendship went back thirty-five years. Brady had thought of going straight to Dr. Peters's home, but this wasn't the time to bring Katie up-to-date with his real background.

"It's only eight-thirty. We can go to Emergency at the medical center and he'll be called in," Brady said.

"No. I did take something. The medicine's going to start working anytime now. I'll be fine. Go home, Brady."

Brady sat down helplessly and looked at the medicine on Katie's nightstand. Cold Plus Flu medication, it said. Should he call Dr. Peters anyway, and ask his advice?

"Would you like some chicken soup?" he asked hopefully. It was what he had been served whenever he was ill.

"No, thank you."

Her quietness bothered him. He hadn't known she was sick sooner, because he'd gone back to his apartment after lunch yesterday to work on a brief. He'd been in court for most of today. In the afternoon, he'd had a meeting with his junior partner to discuss another case coming up soon. It had been seven before he'd gotten to his parents' place and found Mom's note.

Kate suffered through another fit of sneezing. Her streaming eyes and flushed face worried Brady. Restless at the feeling of helplessness that gripped him, Brady's mind chased and discarded endless ideas, before he finally decided he had to do it. He was going to call Dr. Peters.

Five minutes later he was back. Dr. Peters had asked him what medicine Katie was taking. When Brady had named the over-the-counter one on her nightstand, Dr.

Peters had said it was as good as any other, both for the fever and the cold.

Staring down at Katie, Brady noticed her eyes were open. "What's wrong?" he asked.

"I can't stop shaking."

He could warm her with his body, but he didn't think Kate would accept the gesture in the noble spirit it was offered. "Do you have another blanket?"

"No."

Glad to have something to do at last, Brady said, "Be right back."

As soon as she heard the front door close, Kate got up and struggled into her flannel pajamas. Putting her warmest robe on over them, she got back into bed. A minute later she looked at the box on her nightstand. When had she taken her last dose of medicine? Getting up again she dissolved two more tablets in water and drank the fizzy concoction down. Ten minutes later the shivering stopped, and she began to feel drowsy.

Katie awoke feeling better. The medicine must have taken effect, because her nose wasn't all stuffed up. A glance at the cover made her stiffen. A red quilt that looked vaguely familiar lay on top of her own. Sitting up, Kate looked at it and then down at herself. She was wearing a long-sleeved gown. Had she dreamt changing into her flannel pajamas? A glance at the window showed she had actually slept right through the night.

"How are you feeling?"

Kate jumped. What on earth was Brady, tired-looking and in need of a shave, doing here this early?

"You slept here?"

"Yes. Your fever was high and I didn't want to leave you."

"You changed my clothes." Kate took in the pyjamas and robe tossed to one side on the floor.

"Around midnight you got very restless. I came in here to find you drenched with sweat, and very uncomfortable. I couldn't let you stay in those clothes," he said noncommittally.

Kate glared at him, and he could see the anger in her eyes mixed with deep embarrassment.

"You were as helpless as a babe last night, Katie," Brady said quietly, "and I'm no voyeur. I just wanted to make you feel better. If it's any comfort to you, I slipped the nightgown over your head, before I removed your top. You're still wearing the pants."

He stared at the top of Katie's bent head for a minute before adding, "I know what a private person you are, Katie. Stealing what you don't want to give me, even if it's only with a look, isn't my way. I'm as human as the next man, but when I *do* look at you without your clothes, believe me, it will be because you want me to."

Kate felt herself go hot all over. Brady had said *when*, not *if*, as if it were just a matter of time before that happened.

She looked at the bowl of water on her nightstand. It had a small washcloth in it. That hadn't been there when she went to bed. Had Brady been sponging her down, as well? Her fingers began to twist together nervously.

Brady saw her glance at the bowl. "I called Dr. Peters last night. He said a cold water compress on your forehead would help."

"This is Mrs. Guthrie's quilt." No wonder it looked familiar. She'd seen it so many times on the bed in the Guthries' guest room.

Brady nodded. "I was going to buy another one, but when I went downstairs, the Guthries were just pulling up. They introduced themselves. When Mrs. Guthrie heard you were sick, she insisted on lending you her quilt. She also gave me some balm she picked up in Thailand, and told me it worked wonders for a cold if rubbed over the chest and back. Needless to say, I didn't follow her instructions.''

The glint in his eyes told her he would have liked to. Kate's toes began to tingle under the quilt at the images Brady's words painted. Heat worked its way up her body.

''I'll be back in a minute.''

Kate slumped against her pillows as he left the room. She was speechless. Brady could have taken one look at her and left. What had made him stay the night and take care of her?

Her father hadn't cared when Mama was ill, only grumbled about the fact that she couldn't go out and work. *How many times do I have to tell you, Brady isn't your father?* argued her heart. *By staying here and caring for you, he's proved he isn't just a friend to have fun with. He's a man to depend on through good times and bad.*

Remember what Mama told you? A man will say and do anything to get you. Once he's sure of you, then *he shows his true colors.*

Impatience built up in Kate. Brady had never pretended to be anything other than what he was. She'd never seen him as angry as he'd been Sunday, and yet, in some strange way, he'd forgiven her for meddling in his life.

Her eyes fell on the heap of her discarded robe and pajama top. Getting out of bed, Kate picked up the garments and carried them into the bathroom. Brady had more sides to him than she could keep track of.

She came out five minutes later and stared at the plate of toast and scrambled eggs, accompanied by a cup of tea, on her nightstand.

"I'm not hungry."

"Dr. Peters said you wouldn't be, but try and eat something."

"How many times did you call this Dr. Peters?" The man had to be the soul of patience not to mind Brady's intrusion on his time.

Brady grinned. "Thrice."

"Thrice?" Kate stared at him in horror.

He nodded. "Once last night after I got here, once at midnight when you seemed really bad, once this morning at five. The last time, Dr. Peters told me there was a flu epidemic in California, and fifty thousand other people in the state had your identical symptoms, and no, I could not call him the next time you sneezed."

Kate grinned.

Encouraged, Brady added, "He also said he regretted not slapping me harder after he delivered me."

Kate couldn't help laughing at that, though she felt guilty to have caused so much trouble.

"I'm fine."

"No, you're not. Dr. Peters said two people have been hospitalized with severe relapses, because they tried to get back to work too soon. You are to rest and take plenty of fluids."

Giving in was easier than arguing. Kate carried the tray into the living room, ate half a piece of toast and took some more of her medicine while Brady ate the scrambled eggs and reminded her she had to take it easy. Kate retreated to her bedroom, one of her texts tucked under her arm. Ignoring Brady's comments wasn't easy, but she intended to catch up on some studying.

Back in bed, she stared out the window. She'd always been fiercely independent, yet she didn't resent Brady taking care of her. On the other hand, the thought that he had stayed with her through last night, when the going was toughest, stripped her of every defense she had ever put up against the man. A part of her that had never been exposed to his kind of caring before unfurled deep within her, releasing strong messages of longing that confused her.

You're sick, which is why you're imagining all this stuff, pointed out her brain.

Being sick has nothing to do with the fact that you can't stop thinking of Brady, argued her heart. *He's a wonderful person.*

If only, thought Kate, he'd be a little more positive about his attitude where his work was concerned.

The silence told her she was alone when she woke up. A glance at the clock beside her bed showed it was past two o'clock. The sneezing had stopped, but her head felt as if the germs were using it for a landfill. Groaning, Kate dragged herself up and out of bed.

In the kitchen, she found her milk jug filled with a bunch of early freesias from the Guthries' garden. Propped against the jug, was a note.

"Be back soon. Take care."

The words and Brady's signature made Kate's lips curve into a smile of sheer happiness. Hopefully the Guthries wouldn't notice the missing flowers.

In the bathroom, the mirror reflected a face that looked as if it had been made up for Halloween. The dark circles around her eyes would have done a monster credit. Her face was so pale, she could have lost it in a bag of flour. Her nose seemed as red as her hair.

The way she felt didn't match the way she looked. Brady had brought something beautiful to life within her. It flowed through her system like sweet, warm honey.

Her blueprint for Mr. Right had been discarded somewhere. In a daze, she told herself it was silly for her to have ever drawn one up in the first place.

Not trusting herself to go further with *that* train of thought, not in her weakened condition, anyway, Kate turned away, stepped out of her clothes and under a hot shower. She emerged from the bathroom thirty minutes later, head wrapped in a towel, dressed in sweatpants and a T-shirt. Her wobbly legs and spinning head warned her she'd have to take it easy a little longer.

She was asleep when Brady came back. One look at her flushed face and he placed the back of his hand against her forehead.

His touch woke Kate up.

"You're running a fever again." He frowned at the towel still wrapped around her head. "Did you wash your hair?"

"No. I forgot my shower cap, and it got wet in the shower."

Brady's frown grew deeper. "I don't think you're supposed to take showers. Dr. Peters..."

Kate propped herself up on one elbow. "Brady, if you call that poor man one more time on my account, I'll throw you out of here."

"Well, okay," Brady agreed reluctantly, reaching for the towel. Her braids had slipped free of her usual coronet. He started undoing them.

"I can dry my hair later," Kate protested.

Brady issued his own ultimatum. "You have a temperature again. If you don't rest, I'm going to take you into Emergency."

Ignoring her glare, he undid her braids, toweled as much moisture as he could out of her hair, and then fetched the hair dryer and a brush from the bathroom.

"I'll hold the dryer if you want to brush your hair," he said. "When Maura had long hair she always complained that it hurt to have someone else brush it."

Resigned, Kate sat cross-legged on the bed and brushed her hair while Brady held the dryer. As soon as she had the tangles out, he put the dryer down and reached for the brush.

"It reminds me of molten lava, it's so beautiful," he said softly, as he ran the brush through it. He rubbed a strand between thumb and forefinger, enjoying its silken feel.

Kate closed her eyes. The sensations he was creating were at once erotic and peaceful. Rose had loved brushing her hair, telling her its length made her look like a princess. Kate hadn't cut it, simply because of the pleasure it had given her sister.

"I've brought some soup over," Brady said a little later, his voice curiously thick. Seemingly reluctant, he put aside the brush. "You've got to have something."

He returned with a tray, two bowls on it, and said, "I made it myself. It's an old family recipe."

"Brady, why are you doing all this?" Though her heart was telling her that was a silly question, her brain insisted it wasn't. He *was* going beyond the call of friendship.

He looked surprised at her question. "Mom always says sick people have to be cared for. She says half the getting-well process is in the mind, and when a person feels loved, they get better that much quicker."

Kate's breath caught in her throat. Had Rose died because she'd felt unloved?

"What's wrong?" Brady looked at her, quickly picking up on her mood.

"Nothing." Kate forced her mind away from the past. It wouldn't take much to break down and cry in her present state. Then Brady would insist on knowing what was wrong, and she had to avoid revealing her past at all costs. She could imagine his reaction, and the last thing she wanted was his pity.

Brady cupped her face in his hands, turning it upward so she had to look at him. "There are so many secrets in these lovely eyes of yours, Katie. So many. One day I hope you'll share them with me."

Kate's heart did a funny flip-flop, but she said nothing, and Brady let her go, an oddly tender look of patience on his face. Sitting down, he quietly picked up his own bowl of soup and a piece of crusty French bread.

Afraid he might pursue the topic he'd hit on, Kate said quickly, "Brady, tell me about your childhood."

He raised one brow, but complied with her request as soon as his mouth was empty. "My parents came to California from Ireland three years after they were married. Cousin Ellen's husband, Frank, had a grocery business and my father helped him at first. It was about five years before Dad saved up enough money to invest in a furniture shop of his own."

"So, your parents weren't always rich?"

Amazement shot into his eyes. "No. I was fifteen before Dad's business was at a stage where we could even call ourselves a middle-class family. By the time I left college, Dad had opened five branches. He sold the business last year after his bypass surgery."

"You didn't want to take over the family business?" Kate asked.

"No."

When it became obvious Brady wasn't going to say any more, Kate asked, "What do you remember best from your growing-up years, Brady?"

"The love and laughter our house was filled with, and my grandfather's visits from Ireland every other year. Mom and Dad preferred to send him an airline ticket so he could come visit, rather than buy each other Christmas presents. They said Grampy shouldn't miss out on his grandchildren just because we lived in America. Maura and I both learned so much from him."

Brady had been rich even then, thought Kate, a tinge of envy entering her heart. Rich because he'd had a loving home, and parents who cared for each other and believed in family values.

"How was your childhood, Kate?"

"Average."

The answer was flat and noncommittal; she was well aware of that. But she could never share her past with him. Never. A part of her was ashamed of the circumstances surrounding her childhood. How did one explain the bleakness she'd grown up with to a man whose life had been steeped in love and caring?

The silence lasted so long, Brady wondered what was wrong. Taking the bowls back to the kitchen, he returned with the book he'd brought with him. Maybe changing the subject would do the trick.

Kate lay against the pillows, her eyes closed.

"Tired?" he asked gently.

"A bit." She felt drained and achy, like the survivor of a shipwreck. It wasn't only the battle her body was going through that had her feeling like this, it was the turmoil within. The more her mind insisted Brady was Mr. Wrong, the more her heart wanted him.

"Why is marrying a man with money so important to you?" Brady hadn't intended to blurt the question out, but hearing it made him glad he'd gotten it off his chest. He needed to understand, and it was obvious she wasn't going to willingly give him any clues he could use to get through to her. "I mean, you're perfectly capable of making all the money you want in the world yourself."

"I know I am," Kate said fiercely, "but I don't intend to end up like some women do, marrying for love and then supporting a man who's too lazy to work. Besides, I want to be able to stay home and take care of my children when they're young."

Brady stared at Katie, floored by her words and their intensity. As usual, her reasoning had taken him by surprise. She wanted her husband to make enough money, so she could stay home and take care of her children? There was nothing mercenary about that! A weight seemed to lift off his chest and Brady decided he'd been given an inch of hope. And he was going to see if he couldn't get a whole yard more.

"What would you do if you had all the money you wanted in the world?"

"I'd get braces," Kate said matter of factly.

"What?"

There was no mistaking the explosion of incredulous amazement in Brady's voice this time. Kate sighed inwardly, then turned to him. "See this gap in the front?" Baring her teeth, she delicately indicated the gap with the tip of her tongue, making Brady feel the immediate need for a cold shower. "I've always felt awfully self-conscious about it. Wearing braces for a while would close the gap."

Brady's voice shook with the laughter he tried to suppress. She was something else. Didn't she use her mirror? "That gap is beautiful. It makes you look special."

Kate stared at Brady, unable to hide her surprise. What did he mean, special? Every one else who saw it offered to let her have their orthodontist's number.

"I mean it, Katie." When she continued looking at him, clearly unconvinced, he decided to move on. "Besides the braces, and staying home with your kids, what else would you like to do if you had all the money in the world?"

Watching her closely, his stomach tensed. Here it comes, finally, thought Brady. He could tell what was next. The mansion, the diamonds, the fast cars, the jet-set, show-off life-style was undoubtedly what she'd put at the top of the list. Well, it was better to have it out in the open. It would, after all, give him a clearer idea of how to deal with it. And he would, because he'd realized, sometime in the past few worrisome days, that, materialist or not, Katie was the woman for him.

She was quiet for so long, he wondered if she wasn't going to answer.

"I'd like to buy a house in the country. I'd have animals there, and a huge garden and I'd collect children. The children no one wants. Give them somewhere to belong—security, love."

Brady felt his face burn. He swallowed hard. Never, in his wildest dreams, had he anticipated an answer like the one he'd just heard.

Kate blinked. Now what had she gone and said? She had never shared this dream with anyone, and yet when Brady had put that question to her, the answer had seemed to jump out of her mouth, as if launched by a subconscious wish to let him know everything about her.

But shock soon gave way to acceptance. Her words were true. Deep down, in the part of her where only truth existed, that was what she really wanted to do if she ever had all the money she needed in the world. To love the children no one else wanted.

A little dazed yet by her discovery, Kate didn't know why Brady said, "You'll be the death of me, Katie." She looked at him, startled. His voice sounded husky, as if he were choking back laughter. But why?

Brady felt as if he'd found the pot of gold at the end of the rainbow. Her answers proved his gut instincts had been right all along. Katie wasn't mercenary, just a little confused. Brady chuckled, his heart brimming over with warmth. Braces, and a home for children. A woman of unusual ambition was Katie. And there was no way he was letting her get away from him.

He opened the book in his hands. It could only benefit him to keep her off-balance, too. "I'd like to read to you for a bit, if you don't mind."

Her eyes flew open and she looked at the worn leather-bound book in his hands.

"Grampy always read from this book after dinner. It's filled with poems. On his last visit here, he gave it to me," he said simply, loving the look of sweet confusion on her face.

Surprise shot through Kate, that Brady would want to share such a personal part of his life with her. From what he'd told her, she realized he'd been very close to his grandfather.

There was another surprise in store for her. As Brady read, his voice deep and soothing, she discovered that the poetry described a love that exalted men and women's souls, added a wonderful dimension to their lives. Brady's voice brought the words to life, coaxing her to journey with him to the special world where lovers dwelt.

Kate felt the tears gather behind her closed lids. For a few minutes she allowed her imagination full rein. What would it be like to explore that kind of love with Brady?

Absolutely glorious, if one was content only to live for the day without any thought of the future. But she couldn't do that. Brady would never understand her need for security, to have a man who took supporting his family seriously. No, in time her nagging would turn him into another Rip Van Winkle and wreck everything. So it was back to square one. No matter how she felt about Brady, he wasn't the man she could spend the rest of her life with. For her, he would always be Mr. Wrong.

Brady knew exactly when Katie drifted off to sleep, half an hour later. Putting the book down, he tucked her in as if she were Cody's age, before going out to the living room.

Debating whether to leave or stay, he decided to do the dishes and watch the nightly news before he made a decision.

Kate's scream, an hour later, got him on his feet with a jerk. He tore into the bedroom to see her thrashing in the bed, crying, "No, Rose. No. Please don't go."

One arm was stretched out as if reaching for the other person in her nightmare.

Brady put an arm around Kate's shoulders, gathering her to him, while his other hand reached for her outstretched one and brought it to his chest. Close to her ear, he said, "Katie, wake up. It's only a bad dream, sweetheart."

She came out of her nightmare quickly. Opening her eyes, she went very still for a few seconds before she said, "Brady?"

"I'm here, Katie. It was only a nightmare."

Only a nightmare? Kate thought of Rose's face as it had appeared a few minutes ago. Haunted eyes filled with pain, skin stretched across the bones of her once-beautiful face. Kate burst into tears.

"Shh!" Brady rubbed her back and held her while she cried. "You're fine now."

By the time her tears were spent, Kate became aware of two things. Brady's shirt was a mess, and his mouth rested against her temple. His arms were a haven, but she couldn't stay in them forever. They reminded her of what she couldn't have. Placing her hands on his chest, she pushed back. "I'm sorry, I got you all wet."

"I won't shrink." He put a hand up and brushed away a bit of hair stuck to her cheek. "We all need to get things out of our systems once in a while."

Kate grabbed a tissue out of the box Brady placed on the bed and blew her nose. That was it? He wasn't going to question her about the nightmare? He was just going to keep looking at her with sadness lacing those wonderful eyes of his . . . as if the fact that she was upset bothered him deeply. Sparks of heat ignited low in the pit of her stomach. Sharing laughter was easy. Not many people could share another's pain.

Raking a hand through her unbound hair, Kate said the first thing that came into her mind. "I must look like a mess."

Brady frowned as he caressed her cheek with his knuckles. "You're beautiful, Kate."

She froze at the compliment. The heat in her stomach began spreading to other parts of her body. Brady's eyes dropped to her mouth, and she leaned forward into his heat. She needed to be close to him.

The touch of his mouth on her lips unleashed the last of her inhibitions. Sliding closer to him, Kate wound her hands through his hair, silently urging him to increase the pressure of his mouth on hers.

Brady's hungry demands increased as she stoked the fire in him with her own kisses, taking as much as giving, straining for more. His mouth explored her ear and then trailed down her neck. He threaded his fingers through her hair and pulled her even closer. Kate slipped her hands under Brady's shirt, splaying her fingers against the satin of his skin. She shivered with pleasure. Finally, she was touching him the way she'd longed to for so long.

When they both came up for air, she reveled in the thud of his heart beneath her ear. Heart pounding, she only rested there a minute before she raised her face again, sliding her arms around the solid column of his neck, reaching up for his mouth once more.

"Brady," she whispered, "I want you."

Kate felt a great weight leave her as she said the words. The truth released her from the cast iron shackles of secrecy she'd bound herself with. With a jolt, she realized that she didn't *want* to pretend anymore. She wanted Brady Gallagher. And a part of her had already made the decision a couple of weeks ago, because she'd bought protection then.

"Oh, Katie." He kissed her over and over again, each caress more heated than the last.

"Brady, I want you," Kate repeated against his mouth, restless with a desire she couldn't understand fully.

When they broke for air again, a few minutes later, Kate discovered she liked the sensation of Brady lying on top of her. She ran her hands up his shoulders to his face, framing it. An ache throbbed within her and she knew the cure was Brady.

"Make love to me, Brady."

Reason was barred from this room tonight. More than anything, she wanted this one night with the man she now fully admitted her heart had chosen. Tomorrow she would get back on track, return to her search for Mr. Right. But just for tonight, she wanted to forget everything. She was tired of planning and thinking. Tired of analyzing everything she said and did... Tonight she wanted to play hookey from life.

Brady looked at her, down at Kate's passion-filled eyes, and smiled tenderly. He wanted her so badly, he could taste it, but she was in no condition for what they both wanted. He kissed her on the tip of her nose. "Not tonight." He dropped little kisses on her eyebrows, her forehead, her chin, before returning to her lips for another soul-touching kiss. "You're still not completely well, and I never take advantage of the weak. It's one of Brady's laws."

Kate slumped against the pillows as Brady got up and stood beside the bed, tucking his T-shirt back into his pants.

"I think I'll go home, while I still have some willpower left. Are you sure you'll be all right by yourself tonight?"

Kate nodded, still in shock. He was really going to leave?

Another sweet, hot kiss was dropped on her lips, and a few seconds later Kate heard the front door close behind him.

Turning over, she punched her pillow, one thought uppermost in her mind. There were men in this world who thought they knew everything. The I-know-what's-best-for-both-of-us variety. Every single one of them ought to be taken out and shot at dawn. Including Brady.

Chapter Eight

Forty-eight hours later, Kate stared about her, satisfied. A red tablecloth covered the card table. Brass candlesticks in the center held peach-colored candles. She switched off one of the lamps in the living area, content with the romantic glow the other one cast.

Crisp salads waited in the refrigerator. The main course, marinated pork and red cabbage, with its subtle flavoring of spices, was perfect for an evening meal on a warm day. To finish there was chocolate cheesecake. She had ordered the meal at a local deli, and spent most of the day tidying the apartment. She wanted to get everything right this time.

Mrs. Gallagher had called her yesterday and told her they had decided to stay at the beach through the weekend. Cody was having fun, she said, and from what Brady had told them, Kate needed time to recuperate properly.

Kate had talked to Cody for half an hour, reassuring him she was better, and listening to the details of his adventures on the beach. He'd told her he'd be back Monday for sure, and Kate had replied that she was looking forward to spending time with him again.

Talking with Mrs. Gallagher and Cody had helped Kate decide on her now-or-never plan. Calling Brady last night, she'd invited him to dinner. It had been the third time she'd talked with him yesterday. He'd called twice in the course of the day to ask how she was doing. The seductive warmth in his voice had assured Kate she was doing the right thing.

"Tonight," she told the candles, "tonight I'm not tired, or ill or anything. Tonight there are no excuses."

Tonight she would love and be loved.

Kate drew a deep breath and ordered herself to calm down. All day she had alternated between fear at what she was doing, and a heady excitement such as she had never known before. Her brain, for once, had run out of why-not-to reasons.

Three raps on the door, Brady's signature tune, heralded his arrival. Kate squared her shoulders and took a deep breath.

"This is it," she told herself as her trembling legs carried her to the door.

"Hi!" She held on to the door for support after she had opened it.

The fresh soap smell of Brady mixed with a spicy cologne drifted to her, a drugging combination that increased the tremors of her body. His body in the blue slacks and open-necked, paisley silk shirt issued its own invitation to fling herself at him. The strong column of his neck demanded the salute of her lips. He had cut himself shaving, and the sight of the tiny nick above his

mouth made Kate weak with longing. Later, she prom
ised herself, she would kiss it better.

"I missed you, Katie." The words were almost he
undoing. She wanted to abandon dinner and useless sma
talk, throw herself into Brady's arms and demand he lov
her right now.

Why didn't history show any records of women slug
ging and carrying men off, to have their wicked way wit
them? Surely she wasn't the first to want to?

"Please, come in."

"You look well."

That was putting it mildly. Katie looked beautiful to
night. Brady loved the way the white dress she wore clun
to her in all the right places, draping the proud thrust o
her breasts and the soft curve of her hips. The whisper o
the silky fabric, the fragrance of lilacs emanating fron
her, the sight of those gorgeous knees, all combined to
lower whatever resistance he had banked these past forty
eight hours. She had left her hair loose and he loved th
way it framed her face and flowed down her back. The
look in her eyes hinted she wouldn't take no for an an
swer tonight.

Walking closer, Brady told himself it wouldn't be po
lite to say yes immediately. Calmly, he took the bottle o
wine Katie handed him to open. The chilled container fel
good in his hot hands.

All through dinner, their emotions escalated. They
were like two people engaging in some strange matin
ritual. They talked of everything except what was upper
most in both their minds, while their eyes carried on a
different conversation. The candlelight emphasized the
glow of desire in their gazes mixed with the keen edge o
anticipation.

Brady drew his chair close to Katie's when she rose to serve a dessert neither of them wanted to bother with. When she sat down again, his hand closed over her fingers as they reached for her napkin.

"Katie," he whispered, and she melted into his arms.

Their starving lips fused as they slaked their hunger at each other's mouth. Brady stood and drew her out of her chair. Kate went up on her toes, pressing herself against Brady's hard, male warmth. Brady's hands moved on her back, molding her to him. At her response, his hands circled her waist then slowly caressed her rib cage. When they stopped moving for one heart-stopping moment, Kate whimpered a protest. The next instant, Brady's hands cupped her breasts, and Kate's heart threatened to burst out of its bonds.

"Katie," he groaned, dragging his lips from her mouth and burying it in the curve of her fragrant neck.

She pressed his head to her, feeling as if she were going to disintegrate into a million bits of gold dust. Their clothes were an unwanted impediment. Impatient, Kate reached for the buttons of Brady's shirt.

"Katie." He imprisoned her hands against him and looked at her, his eyes doing the asking. Was she really sure about this?

"Yes, Brady," she said, answering his unspoken question, "yes, please."

He picked her up then and carried her into the bedroom. Kate wound her arms around his neck and kissed him passionately. When Brady set her on her feet, Kate sat down on the side of the bed. To her surprise, Brady went down on his knees. The tenderness in his eyes awed Kate as he asked, "Are you sure, Katie?"

"Yes, Brady."

"Katie, I love you." He kissed each creamy shoulder, before trailing his lips down the neck of her dress. The feel of his hot mouth on her sensitive skin was electrifying. When he rested his head against her breasts, Kate's hands pressed his head to her. The explosion of excitement in the pit of her stomach was undeniable.

"I love you, too, Brady," Kate whispered, drowning in the maelstrom of sensation Brady's exploring mouth produced. "That's why I have to have this night to remember."

Brady stiffened as if he'd been shot, and then his hands came up to loosen her arms and return them to her side. He rocked back on his heels and looked at her as he bit out, "Run that by me again."

Katie sank against the pillows and held her arms out to him. "I love you," she repeated with a smile.

He grasped her arms before she could touch him again, and she noticed there was no answering smile on his lips.

"After that," he demanded hoarsely. "What did you say after that?"

"I said I wanted to have this night to remember," Kate repeated. Coming out of her sensual haze, she shivered. Something was wrong. But what? A shaking hand raked through her hair.

"I see." He moved away from her, his anger vibrating in the room. "Might I ask, what the hell you mean? No, let me guess. It's time I took the rose-colored glasses off. You love me, but you still can't marry me because I don't make enough money. So you've decided to make love with me to have something to remember in that rich husband's arms. Am I right?"

He stared at her, and Katie knew he could see the truth in her eyes. Fear turned her blood to ice as she saw the deadly cold front that moved into Brady's eyes, but she couldn't stop herself saying, "I never lied to you about anything, Brady."

He stepped back and said, "Let me look at you." The gray eyes slid over her deliberately, insultingly, "I've seen my share of cold-blooded females, but you take the cake. I don't know how I could have been so wrong, but I was. Well, Miss Langdon, you'll have to find someone else to oblige you. I'm not available in that capacity."

The slam of the door as he left shook her apartment, emphasizing Brady's fury. Her heart and her brain, both in accord for once, told her she'd done the unforgivable.

Kate hadn't realized how irrationally cold-blooded she'd sounded, till Brady had repeated her words. He had every right to be angry. For a second she had wanted to run after him, beg him to listen to her, but she hadn't. It wouldn't do any good.

What could she say to him that would fix what she'd broken?

Brady, I've had a past that's mentioned in psychology textbooks as the worst kind there is. Abuse, poverty, pain, you name it... I've had it.

Or what about—*Brady, I have to fulfill Mama's and Rose's dreams. It's the only way I can make up to them for what they went through. I promised Rose to make something of my life.*

Maybe—*Brady, I didn't plan to use you. Never that. I only wanted to love you and have you love me. I've been alone for so long.*

None of it sounded right. None of it changed anything that had happened. Even the fact that she'd managed to stand up for herself again, in the face of Brady's anger, didn't make her feel better.

Brady had thought she was making a commitment to their future, by agreeing to make love with him. Instinctively she knew that. She had wanted him to love her, because she'd thought it the only way to fill this deep need inside her.

Kate knew she couldn't commit her future to a man so unlike her in every way. It wouldn't be fair. She would want to settle down and Brady would want to sail around the world in a borrowed boat. She would want a bank account and Brady would insist on buying her every pretty thing they saw and charging it to his credit card. It would never last.

On Monday she would tell him about her past. She owed him that much, at least. She had to make him understand why, for her, he was Mr. Wrong.

As dawn streaked the sky, Kate bowed her head on her arms and wept as she recalled the contempt in Brady's eyes. She'd lost something very precious tonight.

Brady watched the sun come up over the ocean from his apartment window. He was tired of it all. Nothing made sense anymore. He had to face up to the fact that the person he'd thought Katie was, and the reality, were two different things.

He had no one but himself to blame. Right from the very beginning, Katie had told him how important financial security was to her, but he had thought he could change things. He'd thought he could show her love was more important, but he'd failed. Chasing a dream, blinded by his own feelings, he'd been unable to accept her for what she was, till she had finally found a way to convince him.

He rubbed a hand over his face.

Though he had all the proof he needed to seal that chapter of his life and write it off as one of his worst failures, he wasn't going to. There was a part of him that still insisted he had to search below the surface for his facts. It was the same part of him that had helped solve his most difficult cases, pushing him to look beyond the obvious, to dig deep for the truth.

Something had made Kate the way she was, and he had to find out what that something was before he bowed out of her life completely.

Was her nightmare some sort of clue? Brady wished he had asked her about it. He hadn't pressed her to tell him anything, because the work he'd done with top psychologists on some of his criminal cases had taught him that forcing someone to face the past could do more harm than good. The best thing was to provide so much security in the present that past fears lost their hold on a person. Besides, after the nightmare, his main concern had been to comfort Katie, not force her to face what had so obviously terrified her.

He dropped his head into his hands. He had given Katie just about as much as one human being was capable of giving another.

"It's not giving that empties the purse, nor lovin' that empties the heart."

Brady's head shot up. It was uncanny he should remember that quotation scrawled on the flyleaf of the book he'd been given. He couldn't count the times Grampy had read the words to both him and Maura.

Now, as Brady watched the sunbeams dance on the water, it seemed like the reminder had come just in time. The conviction that Katie and he were made for each other returned as strong as the rising sun.

He loved everything about her: her spirit, her warmth, even her doggone stubbornness. He had to try to work things out. Giving up now would be like quitting on his own dreams. And that was something he wasn't about to do.

Brady dropped Cody off at the condominium at eight on Monday, because he had to be in court by ten. A quick look at Katie showed she looked paler than normal. His heart lurched but he knew now wasn't the time to tackle any discussions.

"Brady, I need to talk to you," she said, as soon as Cody had raced up to his room.

He looked at her without saying anything, and she saw the lingering anger in his eyes. Grief tearing her apart inside, Kate looked over her shoulder to make sure Cody was still out of hearing range. "Could we go to the park or something tonight?"

"I can't today. I have an appointment after work."

"I . . . see." Her heart plummeted. He didn't want to have anything more to do with her. "I'll see you later, then."

"Later."

The quiver of her lips as she tried to stretch them into a smile hurt.

As he walked to his car, Brady told himself there was no reason on earth for him to feel guilty. But he did. He should have told Kate he'd meet her this evening, but parts of him were still raw, his anger still emitting sparks. He needed a little more time to himself.

"There's a doggy outside the window, Kate," Cody said half an hour later.

He was on a chair by the sink, helping her dry their breakfast dishes.

Kate joined him at the kitchen window and saw the small, black puppy sniffing hopefully around the bushes in front. As they watched, he ran to the end of the drive, and then came back.

"Maybe he's just out for a run," Kate suggested, looking to see if his owner was in sight.

The rain that had started at midnight had let up half an hour ago. Maybe someone was walking the dog. But the road stretched empty on either side and Kate wondered if someone had let the pup out by himself. He looked too small to be out on his own.

"Why's he crying if he's just out for a run?" Cody's voice reflected deep concern.

Kate could hear the whining clearly.

"Is he lost?" asked Cody anxiously.

Kate came to stand beside him. "He might be. Let's wait ten minutes and see." Pointing to the clock on the kitchen wall she said, "Ten minutes will be over when the large hand comes to eight."

Cody remained on the chair, his eyes wandering from the puppy to the clock, while Kate vacuumed the family room, wondering if Brady would ever forgive her.

She hadn't liked the way his eyes had held no expression at all as he'd looked at her this morning. It had been like looking at a stranger. Kate felt a storm of tears coming on and bit her lip.

She couldn't play dog in the manger with Brady. He deserved better.

All weekend she had gone over and over everything that had happened, but she kept coming back to the same point. Brady wasn't the marrying kind; how could she have done any different than she had?

"The puppy's gone," Cody announced.

"That means he wasn't lost."

Kate passed the morning playing with Cody and listening to the story of his week at the beach. He had talked to his mother and father twice. They missed him, and they were going to bring him back a huge koala bear.

All morning long, Cody kept climbing on the chair by the kitchen window to check for the black puppy. It had disappeared, and Kate hoped its owner had found it.

At two, when Cody woke up from his nap and sat at the table with a glass of milk and cookies in front of him, they both heard an unmistakable howl.

"It's the doggy." Cody raced to the window. "He's back, Kate, he's back."

And he had a limp, as well, now.

"Is he hurt?" asked Cody.

"We'd better check."

If the puppy had been running around all morning, it must be starving. Its fur was matted with mud and it looked miserable. Kate headed for the garage, Cody close on her heels.

"Stand back, Cody," she warned, as she pressed the button that operated the garage door opener. The puppy bounded in. "I have to check him out first."

Licking her hand as if he knew her, the puppy's tail wagged nineteen to the dozen while Kate searched the fur around his neck for a collar and identity tag. There was nothing on the little cocker spaniel except a bedraggled red ribbon.

"I'd better get him a slice of bread, soaked in milk. He looks hungry."

The puppy lapped at the meal ravenously and Kate realized it probably hadn't had anything to eat all day.

"Kate, may I touch him now?" As Cody was already having his hand licked, there was nothing Kate could do but agree.

The sound of an approaching car made the puppy cower closer to the little boy. Kate's heart thudded as Brady got out of the BMW. What on earth was he doing back so early?

"Who's our friend?" he asked.

The dog, sensing another sympathizer, bounded over to him immediately. Kate envied the puppy the smile it received. All she'd been given was an unnerving, searching stare.

"Uncle Brady, he's lost." Cody sounded ready to cry. "Kate says the storm frightened him and so he ran away 'n now he can't find his way home. Do you know where he lives, Uncle Brady?"

"I'm afraid not, buddy." Brady glanced at Katie, who seemed fascinated by the cracks in the garage floor. "Have you called the Humane Society, Katie?"

"Not yet." Kate knew it was what she'd have to do eventually.

Without the puppy having any identification, all the Humane Society could do was board the animal and wait awhile for someone to claim it. If it wasn't picked up within a certain time, it would be put to sleep. Kate didn't like the thought.

"Maybe if we wait awhile . . ." Her eyes pleaded with Brady to understand.

"How long has it been here?"

"We saw him soon after you left this morning," Kate said slowly.

"We have to call the Humane Society, Katie," said Brady gently. "Maybe the owners are already looking for it."

He turned to go indoors.

Maybe not, thought Kate rebelliously. *Maybe he's just another mixed-up stray like me.*

The officer that came out from the Humane Society was very pleasant. Picking up the pup, the woman confirmed Kate's opinion that it was a purebred cocker spaniel. Nobody had reported him missing, but she'd call the other Humane Society branch twenty miles away and check.

"Would you let us know if someone comes for him, please?" Kate hated to see the pup go.

"He'll be fine," Brady said quietly as the van disappeared.

"Have you ever been to an animal shelter, Brady?" Kate demanded fiercely. "Do you know what happens to the dogs if they can't find homes for them?"

Turning away without waiting for an answer, Kate went indoors, her throat tight with tears.

Following behind her, she heard Cody ask, "Uncle Brady, what do they do to the dogs if they can't find their homes?"

Let him explain his way out of that one, Kate thought with satisfaction. Gathering her things, she reached for her jacket in the closet when she heard Brady say, "We could make notices about the pup being found, and put them up around Jacaranda Meadows and by the grocery store. The owner's sure to see one of them."

"I thought you had an appointment this evening?" Kate asked quietly.

"This is more important." Brady's eyes seemed to send another message as they delved deeply into hers.

"All right." Kate smiled for the first time that day. "Let's make posters."

"Let's make posters," echoed an excited Cody.

While he booted Jack's computer, Brady stared at Katie and Cody, discussing what to put on the sign. Haunted all day by the deep sadness he'd glimpsed in Katie's eyes that morning, Brady hadn't been able to do a lick of work. He'd left the office early, asking his secretary to call and cancel his five o'clock appointment. His client was very important, but no one took precedence over Kate.

After he printed the signs, Kate and Cody glued the sheets of paper to cardboard, and then Kate outlined the words *PUPPY FOUND* with a red marker. The first three signs were hung on poles by the main entrances to Jacaranda Meadows, and the last one by the front door of the grocery store.

"I'm going to sit by the phone and wait for them to call," Cody announced as soon as the last poster had been put up.

Over his head, Brady's gaze met Kate's. It was going to be a long evening if he couldn't come up with something to distract his nephew, and quick.

"Grandpa's going to answer the telephone. I told him about the pup. How would you like to see the new Walt Disney movie at the mall?" he asked. By the time the movie was finished, he was sure Cody would be half-asleep.

Cody's eyes lit up. He looked at Kate. "Want to see the new Walt Disney movie at the mall, Kate?" he asked.

She looked at her watch. The poster project had kept her so busy, she hadn't realized she was late for class. "What about your appointment?" she reminded Brady. "I can take Cody to the movies."

"I realized my first priority was talking to you, so I postponed it."

Some of the ice around Kate's heart cracked and began to melt. Brady hadn't stayed on just to reassure Cody. He'd come back to talk to her.

She glanced from Cody's expectant expression to Brady's watchful one. They wouldn't get much of a chance to talk, but she wanted to be with Brady.

"I'll come," she said.

Chapter Nine

The nightmare returned that night. The faces that always made her feel bad were there. Rose's tear-filled eyes, Mama's bearing the stamp of untold suffering, her father's angry ones. Fear built within her, and Kate opened her mouth to scream.

But instead of the terror escalating as it always did, Kate felt strong arms go around her. Brady's voice whispered into her ear, "You're safe with me, Kate."

She burrowed into his chest, seeking more of his warmth. With him, she would always be safe. Always. She lifted her face for a kiss and when nothing happened, she opened her eyes. She was alone in her bedroom.

Sitting up, Kate wrapped her arms around herself, the sense of Brady's presence still with her. Even in her dreams it had become more powerful than any of her old fears.

"Brady."

The word left Kate's lips, a plea that contained all her pent-up longing.

She loved Brady.

No matter what similarities he had to her father and Rose's boyfriend on the surface, Brady was different inside. Look at the way he had canceled his appointment yesterday, to give her a chance to talk to him. True, they hadn't gotten around to it, but it was the thought that counted. In spite of all she'd done and said, he still cared. He had also guessed, without being told, how upset she'd been over the lost puppy, and he'd gone out of his way to help make and put up the posters. He would never let her down. He was kind and sensitive . . . indestructible qualities that nothing would ever change. He might have a cavalier attitude toward work, but he would never let her, or any children they had, want for anything.

She fell asleep again in the early hours of the morning, her decision made. Today she would tell Brady she loved him.

Mrs. Gallagher called at eight the next morning to ask Kate if she would mind picking Cody up. Brady had left early for work, and she had a dentist's appointment at nine.

Which only meant, Kate thought, as she picked Cody up at his grandparents' house and drove to the condominium, that telling Brady she loved him would have to be put off for a few more hours. She ignored her disappointment and impatience. Her mind could use the time rehearsing what she'd say.

She'd dressed with extra care that morning, choosing a silk blouse in her favorite aqua color, and black jeans. Her reflection in the mirror that hung in the Brighams' entryway made Kate glad that her job at the department store had enabled her to put together a really nice wardrobe. She still went back and shopped there occasionally, and an old girlfriend saw to it that she got a discount on her purchases.

"Kate, do you think someone saw our notices?"

"I don't know, Cody."

"Maybe they fell off or somethin'."

"Nope, they're there. I saw three on my way to pick you up. I'm sure someone's going to call today."

Temporarily satisfied, Cody agreed to Kate's suggestion that they wait till noon before calling the Humane Society for news.

Brady had put both his sister's and his parents' telephone number on the flyer. Kate and Cody were finger painting when the telephone rang at eleven. After she'd hung up, she turned to Cody, her eyes shining. "That was from the puppy's owners. They've been very sad since he ran away. They picked him up at the Humane Society and they called to say thank-you for being nice to him and for putting up the signs."

Cody's eyes lit up. "He must be happy now," he stated.

"He's very happy. They told me his name is Jolly."

"When I get a puppy, I'm going to call him Jolly, too," Cody said, going back to his picture.

Kate smiled, then she stared at her own sheet. Like a moony teenager, she'd painted an enormous heart and put the initials K and B inside. Looking at it, Kate felt she couldn't wait till five to see Brady.

The morning's cloudy skies gave way to a downpour at noon, adding to her restlessness. Picking up on her mood, Cody turned down all her ideas of things they could do, until she suggested a game of dress-up.

His eyes bright with enthusiasm, he said, "I'm going to be Uncle Brady."

Racing up the stairs, he returned with a black silk dressing gown of his mother's. In an effort to humor him, Kate let him help her into the gown. Tying the belt around her middle she asked, "Who am I supposed to be?"

Cody looked surprised. "You're the judge."

"I see." Had Brady gotten a traffic ticket, or something, recently?

"I'm going to tell the judge to send all the bad guys to jail. I'm the 'torney," Cody announced.

Kate thought she was familiar with Cody's speech, but the last word was a new one she hadn't heard before.

"I have to give you this, so you'll know who I am." Taking a small box from the backpack he brought with him every day, Cody handed her a business card.

Kate glanced at it, wondering if he'd gotten into his father's stuff, and her eyes widened.

It read Brady J. Gallagher, Attorney At Law.

Shock made the address below the first two lines blur.

Kate looked up. "You're a lawyer," she said blankly.

Cody nodded impatiently. "I *told* you. Just like Uncle Brady. Mom 'n Dad 'n me went to a big courthouse once to see him talk to a judge. Can we start now?"

Kate had no idea of what she said or did in the next half hour, but her mechanical responses didn't bother Cody. He incorporated superhero tactics into his game, his imagination providing sufficient company for his play acting.

Brady was a lawyer. The BMW, the boat, the classic elegance of his clothes—everything fell into place. No wonder he spent money like water. He had plenty of money. He had just chosen not to tell her so.

A derisive smile lifted one corner of Kate's mouth as she thought of the salesman act he'd put on. It was all so clear now. Bernie's Gifts and Luggage must belong to his mother, Bernice Gallagher. Kate just hadn't figured it out because Mr. Gallagher always called his wife Berry. She had never seen Mrs. Gallagher in the store, but she'd only been there twice...once to look for Harold's present, the second time to buy it.

Her heart felt as if it were shriveling. She couldn't blame Brady for not telling her the truth. He had a right to his views just as she had hers. He had wanted to marry someone who could love him for himself, not for what he had.

What a fool she'd been to put off telling him she loved him. Now it was too late. After all that happened, he would never believe she truly loved him for himself. As far as ironies went, this latest twist was one of the worst punches life could have landed her.

Scenes with Brady came back to haunt her. That first time in the store. Had she known love then and not been able to recognize it? She'd been so blind.

There were so many other times. At the zoo, when he'd first kissed her. On the boat, where he had kept his word, and proved what a good friend he could be. Then there was the look in his eyes when he'd seen Cody fall asleep as she'd read to him. She'd run away from his affection, measuring him against men who couldn't hold a candle to him.

The way he'd cared for her when she'd been ill had proved how unselfish he was, that he would put her well-being above all else. He'd even refused to take advantage of her when she was sick ... and in return she'd hurt him badly.

Why had she held on to her stupid plans for so long? When it came to lost opportunities, she, Kate Langdon, had missed the boat, the steamer and the *Queen Elizabeth*.

A million fragmented shards arose and pieced themselves together, till Kate had a picture in front of her eyes of a man, one in a million. A man any woman would be proud to love. He'd told her his love alone would provide her with all the security she ever needed. And he'd shown her in a thousand ways that he would care for her, no matter what, but she had fallen short on faith. In Brady's book, love accompanied responsibility.

He'd held the key to their happiness in his cupped hands, waiting for the right moment to give it to her. She'd snatched it from his hands and tossed it away.

Cody answered the doorbell when Brady rang it at five. Something in Kate's gaze as she said hello warned Brady all was not as it should be. His gaze fell from her face to the business cards scattered on top of the coffee table. *His* business cards. Cody must have taken them out of his briefcase yesterday.

The muscles of his stomach twisted into a knot. His gaze shot back to her. He'd never intended for Katie to find out this way.

"Get the stuff you want to take to Grandma's, buddy."

As soon as Cody disappeared, Brady sat down beside Kate. In a low voice, he said, "I'm sorry, Katie. I meant to tell you."

"It's all right."

He wished she'd yell at him. Her quietness made him terribly uneasy. She lifted her blank gaze to him, and the emptiness he glimpsed there was like a slap in the face.

"A part of me, the part that's still romantic Irish wanted you to love me for myself, Katie," he explained quickly. "That was the only reason I lied to you."

She stood up and began to collect her things. "I said, it's all right, Brady. Don't worry about it."

"Dammit Katie, it's *not* all right. If you weren't the stubbornest woman in the world, you'd listen to me—"

"Bye, Brady." The door closed noiselessly behind her.

Brady stared after her, feeling like a total idiot.

Cody rushed down the stairs and looked around for Kate. "I didn't say 'bye to Kate," he said.

"Kate was late for her class," Brady said quickly.

Cody frowned at him. "She doesn't have a class today. It's Toosday."

Brady sighed. "Well, she was late for something, and she'll tell you what tomorrow."

All evening, Brady stewed over what had happened. As soon as his mother returned from the store, he left for his own apartment, saying he had a brief to prepare. He wanted to nurse his wounds in private.

Women. Katie could at least have listened to him. What right did she have to judge him, anyway? It was partly her fault for being too darn stubborn to admit how important love was.

From time to time he'd been tempted to try Plan X. Every other plan had backfired. Plan X had been to tell her he was rich, marry her and *then* convince her how important love was. But Brady knew he couldn't have done that. If he had married her on those grounds, in time his own insecurities would have corroded his relationship with Katie. Too many women had chased him for *what* he had, not who he was, for him to ever take that risk.

He'd have to come up with yet another plan, or concede he couldn't keep fighting Katie.

The call Saturday afternoon took Kate by surprise.

"Kate, we're back."

"Maura?" Kate hazarded a guess over the wire. The Brighams weren't due back for another two weeks.

"Yes. We just couldn't stay away from Cody any longer. Jack worked around the clock last week to finish the most important stuff, and here we are. Everyone was surprised when we walked through the front door an hour ago."

"I'll bet they were." Kate wondered if "everyone" included Brady, as well. She hadn't seen him since last Tuesday. Approximately three days, sixteen hours and forty-five minutes, but who was counting? She had to get used to it sooner or later.

She'd taken Cody to Disneyland on Thursday, the arboretum yesterday. But no matter what she did, she hadn't been able to stop thinking of Brady.

"We can't thank you enough. I hope Cody wasn't too much trouble," Maura went on. "He can't stop talking about you. Finding you was the best thing that happened to us. We can't believe the change in him. He's filled out and seems like such a big boy now. And we were so proud when he picked up his book and read the story of the green bunny to us. Mom says it's all your doing."

"I enjoyed watching him. He's a great kid." Teaching Cody to sound letters phonetically hadn't been difficult, as he already knew his alphabet.

"I'd like to see you tomorrow, if that's all right with you. We must catch up on all the news."

"Of course," Kate mumbled. "I'm free in the morning."

It hit her suddenly that she no longer had a job. Worse, she no longer had any reason for seeing Brady. Which idiot had said a clean break was the best kind there was? This one hurt more than anything she had ever experienced. The fact she'd only known him six weeks didn't make a difference. Time couldn't be used as a factor to measure how much one cared about a person. Her heart felt heavy with the knowledge she wouldn't be seeing Brady again. What was she going to do without him?

Kate rang the bell of the Brighams' condominium at exactly ten the next morning. Maura's greeting surprised her. Cody's mother put her arms around her and hugged her as if she were a dear friend, talking nonstop, as usual.

"I can never thank you enough for all you did for us. We love the book Cody made for us. It was so thoughtful of you to take a Polaroid picture of him each week, for us."

They sat in the kitchen, had coffee and talked about the trip and Cody for a while, before Maura excused herself and went into the family room, to return with a check and a gift-wrapped package.

"You don't owe me anything," Kate protested. "Your mom paid me on Friday."

"We do, too," said Maura, placing the gift and check in front of Kate. "Jack and I don't want you to refuse this. It's payment for the next two weeks with a small bonus."

Kate's eyes widened as she peeked at the check. Maura's idea of a "small" bonus was another two weeks' salary. "It's too much."

"It's not. We did hire you for eight weeks and this should help till you find another job. We really owe you more than money can ever repay." Maura's gaze went to

the package. "I picked up something small for you i
Sydney. I hope you'll like it."

Loving just came naturally to the Brighams and th
Gallaghers. Kate felt her throat clog. "Thank you." Sh
stood up before she could disgrace herself by crying i
front of Maura. She'd open the present later, when sh
was by herself. "I have to go now. I have an appoint
ment in Los Angeles."

"Cody's gone to the store with Brady and Jack. He'
be sorry he missed you, but may he call you later? W
want to keep seeing you. Our new house will be ready i
six weeks, and I want you to come to our housewarmin
party."

Kate nodded. "I'd like that. Tell Cody I'll be home b
five."

Brady had been outside his sister's condo for the pa
ten minutes. Jack and Cody had decided to go to the par
for a while. Brady had returned because he wanted t
visit Katie and tell her that he loved her. The sight of he
car here had been a surprise. Why was she here? Ram
ming his hands into the pockets of his slacks, Brad
stared at Maura's front door.

It had been bad enough in the beginning, when he'
asked Maura and Mom not to mention he was a lawyer
They had teased him then, but now things were eve
worse. Ever since Maura's return, she and Mom had bee
making very pointed remarks about Katie. They wer
dying to know everything that was happening. It woul
take only a few minutes in the company of his shrew
sister for Maura to put two and two together and com
up with the fact that he was head over heels in love wit
Katie.

He didn't want Maura meddling in his love life.

Not seeing Katie these past few days had been the hardest thing he had ever done. And staying away had convinced him that he loved Katie more now than he had ever before. She'd had more than enough time to get over being angry with him. He meant to straighten everything out today.

"Brady!"

He turned at Kate's gasp. "Hello, Kate." Was it his imagination or did she look paler than usual? It could be that black shirt she was wearing, though.

"How are you?" She walked to her car and opened the door on the driver's side as she asked the polite question. He could have been a casual acquaintance; someone she barely knew. Maura stood at the door of the condominium, silently glancing from Kate to Brady.

Brady frowned as Kate got into her car and slammed the door. How dare she act like a stranger? He took a step forward, and then stopped. Instead of roaring to life, the engine wheezed and died. A smile lifted the corner of Brady's mouth. His luck hadn't deserted him entirely.

She tried to start the car two more times, before she opened the door.

"May I use your phone?" she asked Maura, ignoring him. "It's probably the battery again."

"Oh, Brady can look at it for you," Maura said quickly. "He won't mind, will you, Brady?"

Plan Y was beginning to take root in his mind. As Kate paused by Maura, Brady strode over to the car and propped the hood open, recalling the time it hadn't started that first day. Bending, he pretended to conduct a detailed examination.

"Does it need a jump start?" Kate asked, when she couldn't stand the silence any longer.

Brady closed the hood quickly. "I'm afraid you're going to have to call a tow truck. It's the alternator belt."

"What's wrong with it?" Exasperation warred with her need to get away, before she broke down completely in front of Brady. Why hadn't she sandwiched an auto-shop class between the dancing and swimming lessons?

"It's snapped."

Kate closed her eyes for a second. It sounded terribly expensive.

"Does this mean you'll have to cancel your appointment?" Maura asked.

Kate bit her lip. The thought of her former teacher, eighty-four year old Mrs. Henry, sitting alone in her room at the Hillside nursing home, wondering if someone would show up to wish her a happy birthday was more than she could stand.

"If you don't mind my leaving the car here, I'll call a tow truck later," Kate said. Waiting for one now could take an hour or longer. It was more important not to keep Mrs. Henry waiting. "May I use your telephone to call a cab?"

"You're going to take a cab all the way to Los Angeles?" Maura asked.

Before Kate could reply that she only intended to take the cab as far as the nearest bus terminal, Brady said, "I could give you a ride."

Maura beamed. "Of course. That's the perfect solution."

"I don't want to take you away from your family," Kate said hesitantly.

"Oh, we don't mind," said Maura quickly. "We all stayed up half the night talking."

"I don't have any plans for today. I'd be glad to take you," Brady added, thanking the gods for their intervention.

Kate could hardly refuse, without making Maura wonder what was wrong. "Thank you, Brady."

Getting the gift she'd bought Mrs. Henry, her handbag and another package out of the back seat, Kate walked over to Brady's car.

He was on the freeway, when she said, "If you'll just drop me off at the bus terminal, I can take a bus."

"Relax, Katie. A forty-five minute drive's not going to ruin my day."

Kate sank back in her seat. Brady sounded curt and unfriendly. Clutching her gift to her chest, she reminded herself she was doing this for Mrs. Henry. Now if only she could ignore the way her body was reacting to being so close to Brady once again.

"Have you found another job?" Brady asked after a while."

"Not yet."

"My friend's offer is still open."

"Stay out of my personal life, Brady," Kate said as evenly as possible, recalling the offer he'd made of an office job when they'd first met.

"I'm only trying to help you find a man who will give you the financial security you need."

Kate bit her lip.

"What happened to Harold?"

"Harold?" Kate repeated, surprised. "I haven't seen him since his birthday."

The silence that followed reminded Kate that liars needed great memories.

"Then what was all that about going out to dinner with Harold and thinking about spending the weekend with him?" Brady's voice was deadly quiet.

Kate rubbed her neck. "I needed protection from you, Brady."

"You lied to me," he yelled, forgetting his promise not to.

"You lied to me, too, about being a salesman," Kate yelled back, angrier than she had ever been. "Why is it all right for you to lie, but not for me?"

Brady was so angry, he couldn't speak. She had deliberately caused him grief. Thinking of all the time he'd spent planning how to cut Harold out of Kate's life made him even angrier.

The discovery that she'd yelled back at Brady, and that she fully intended to repeat the procedure if he raised his voice again, surprised Kate. She wasn't meek like...like...

Kate raised a hand to her mouth. She'd been about to say, like Mama and Rose. Staring blankly ahead, she realized it was true. They'd accepted everything doled out to them, but she was a fighter. For the first time, Kate began to wonder if Rose had ever stood up to the man she had run away with. Had her sister followed in their mother's footsteps, accepting all the blows, believing she couldn't do anything else?

Kate bit her lip. Mama had never said a word in her own defense. Why had Rose, the outspoken one at home, taken after their mother when it came to accepting ill-treatment? Every woman had a right to let a man know he couldn't go beyond certain boundaries of behavior. A right to stand up for herself.

Her reaction—in the past and today—proved to Kate she had the ability to stand up for herself. Her life wasn't going to be a rerun of Mama's or Rose's, simply because she wasn't as passive as they had been. Loving Brady had increased her own self-esteem, given her courage. With his unconditional acceptance of her, his understanding, he had helped her develop her inner confidence.

She wasn't scared of him . . . not in the way Mama had been afraid of Chuck Langdon. Brady would never think of being physically violent with her. He was too special to ever condone behavior like that.

"Where are we going?" Brady asked, when they were ten minutes away from Los Angeles.

"Hillside Nursing Home." Kate told Brady which exit he'd have to take.

"Visiting a relative?"

"No. Mrs. Henry's an old friend." For some reason Kate was reluctant to mention Mrs. Henry had been her teacher.

When they reached the exit, Kate gave Brady directions. As they got to the street on which the nursing home was, she said, "Would you mind dropping me off at the bakery at the corner? Thank you for the ride, Brady."

She had to pick up the cake she had ordered for Mrs. Henry, and from the bakery it was only a short walk to the nursing home.

Brady looked around him. Surprise had held him silent for the past ten minutes as they'd entered this area. The neighborhood was questionable, and he didn't like the men standing at the corner, staring at the car. He had no intention of abandoning Katie here.

"How do you propose to get home? Fly?" Uneasiness lent an edge to Brady's tone. What on earth was Katie's friend doing in a nursing home in this part of Los Angeles?

"There's a bus stop a couple of blocks from Hillside. I'll catch a bus to Anaheim from there, and then take a cab home."

Kate's tone was as confident as if she were discussing a walk in the park, back in Jacaranda Meadows.

"Thanks, Brady," Kate repeated as he brought the car to a halt.

He got out just as Kate did. She stared at him in surprise over the top of the car as he slammed his door, locked it and said, "I'm coming with you."

He waited as she paid for the huge cake she'd ordered, and then carried it out to the car for her.

When they reached Hillside, he pulled into the visitor's parking lot and said, "Go ahead and visit for as long as you like. I've got some papers to go through. I'll be over there."

He jerked his head to a grassy patch near the lot with a few picnic benches on it.

Kate hesitated for just a minute before she said, "I'd like you to come and meet Mrs. Henry."

Brady looked at her in surprise. "Are you sure?"

Kate nodded. "I'm sure."

As they entered the building and she led the way to Mrs. Henry's room, Kate wondered what her ex-teacher was going to make of Brady. Very little ever escaped Mrs. Henry.

Ten minutes later Brady watched quietly as Katie and Arletha Henry chatted. It was obvious Katie was very attached to the older woman. He'd been surprised by the things she'd brought for her. Books, a sweater, fruit and a box of chocolates, besides the yet-unopened present. The cake had cost quite a bit, too. He'd heard Mrs. Henry thanking her for sending money to help an old school friend whose husband had left her. The time she mentioned had been when Kate had just started watching Cody. She'd been out of work for a while, and she'd still sent almost her entire first paycheck to help someone?

He'd never doubted Katie's generosity. His mom had mentioned the fact Katie hadn't turned in any bills for the craft items or the other things she'd bought for Cody. But this went beyond regular generosity. His heart swelled with love.

Katie would be a generous lover, too, holding nothing back, giving as much as she got. The memory of her with the white dress pushed off her shoulders, her face flushed from his kisses, made Brady's hands clench at his sides. If only he could convince her that loving and commitment went hand in hand.

Chapter Ten

"So you're Kate's man?"

Brady's brow went up. Katie had gone off in search of matches to light the candles on Mrs. Henry's cake.

"No one deserves happiness more than that girl."

"Have you known Kate long?" he asked.

"Ever since she was in my ninth-grade class."

"You're her teacher?" Brady couldn't disguise his surprise.

"Didn't she tell you?" The black eyes studied him as one shaking hand reached up and patted the corkscrew white curls. "I taught English to high school students for thirty-three years."

"She didn't mention it."

"Well, maybe I should mind my own business and let you both work it out, but then I'm not going to. At my age, I can see when two people are in love, but aren't doing anything about it. And I know people shouldn't waste either time, or a gift as precious as love. Especially when they've starved all their lives without the latter, like my Kate."

Brady didn't say anything, just nodded again. Mrs. Henry obviously knew something he didn't, and he wasn't going to stop her from giving him the ammo he needed.

"You look like a smart lad, so I'll give you one hint." Mrs. Henry looked at the door quickly. "Kate grew up around here. The high school she went to is just around the corner. Any of the tenement buildings you passed between the bakery and this place could have been her home."

Brady took a deep breath. He'd had strange facts thrown in his face before, but this took the prize.

Kate returned before he could say a word, with a few of the staff in tow. They sang "Happy Birthday" and after the cake was cut and he'd eaten a piece, Brady told Kate he'd be outside and slipped away. As he left, a few more people entered the room, attracted by the noise and laughter.

It was a while before all Mrs. Henry's friends left. Kate stared at the white frosting she hadn't eaten on her plate. She had that old familiar feeling that Mrs. Henry was about to speak her mind.

She didn't have to wait very long. "You might have got all A's in my class girl, but right now I'll give you a D– for stubbornness."

Kate looked up as Mrs. Henry continued. "You've got a good man, whose eyes catch fire every time he looks at you, and what are you doing? Pretending there's nothing going on between you. Now don't tell me you're not comparing him to that no-good father of yours, and that man your sister ran off with, because I know the way your mind works. Both your mama and Rose had their chances. This is yours. You can't pay your whole life for what happened to them. You're different, Kate. Stronger, and more intelligent. You won't turn into your mama, or Rose.''

Mrs. Henry's words were all the prompting Kate needed to tell her about the mess she'd made of everything.

Mrs. Henry shook her head when Kate stopped talking. "You can't tell Brady you love him because you're still thinking too much. Let your heart lead you the rest of the way. Remember what the school psychologist told you? Let the past go, Kate. It robbed you of your girlhood—don't let it have the rest of your life, as well.''

The bell signaling the end of visiting hours brought Kate to her feet. She'd been here longer than she'd intended.

"The next time you come to see me it better be with a wedding invitation in your hand." Mrs. Henry's voice was as strict as when she'd announced detentions in ninth grade, but her eyes were damp. When Kate hugged her, the older woman held her as tight as her thin arms would allow.

"I'll call you, and I'll see you in two weeks," Kate said before she went to look for Brady.

She felt reluctant about taking Mrs. Henry's advice and telling Brady about the past. Except for her teacher and the school psychologist, Kate had never talked to anyone about her roots. It was too painful. But maybe...

Walking the grounds at Hillside had helped Brady reach one conclusion. He was what Grampy would have called "a body without a head on his shoulders.''

Arletha Henry's words had made so much fall into place. He had judged Kate without walking in her shoes for a while. How could he have been so blind? He had seen only his point of view, thought only of what he considered marriage deserved. He was selfish, pompous and so full of hindsight, he could write a book entitled *How Not To Make a Mess of Your Love Life.*

When Kate came out from her visit, she made no attempt to break the silence, not even as they drove back. Mrs. Henry's words still rang in her mind.

Let the past go . . . don't let it have the rest of your life.

But she had. Fear had forced her to throw Brady's love away. Too late she had discovered that love never came with any insurance, but that if one didn't reach for love with faith, one would always remain poor in the worst possible sense.

She had been so busy standing in Mama's and Rose's shadows, she hadn't recognized her own worth as a woman. True, she and Rose had been raised in the same home, but her way of thinking, and her approach to life, were worlds apart from Rose's.

Immersed in her thoughts, Kate looked up in surprise when the car stopped. They weren't anywhere close to the Guthries' house. Brady had pulled up in a section of the park that overlooked the golf course.

She turned to him, uneasily wondering what Brady wanted to discuss.

There were a hundred things he could say. He could tell her he understood. He could apologize for his tunnel vision. He could beg for forgiveness. The words that popped out of his mouth, though, surprised him. "Who is Rose?"

It was the name she had cried out in her nightmare.

Kate realized she had nothing to lose by telling Brady about her past. Suddenly Rose seemed as good a starting point as any. If Brady could understand her, then maybe he would forgive Kate for what she'd done to him.

Staring out of the windshield, she gathered her strength and began, "Rose was my sister. She looked out for me, took me out of harm's way when my father got drunk and abusive. She used to tell me stories, and brush my hair. When our father...hit Mama, Rose told me we were never going to let any man do that to us. Never. We were going to study and be very smart, and one day we would marry men who were rich. We would live in nice houses, and our kids would have toys to play with."

Kate paused and swallowed hard to hold back the tears stinging her eyes. It was difficult, but she was proud that when she continued, her voice was even, fairly unemotional. "When my father left us, Rose changed. She started staying out late. One day she brought this man home to meet me. Rose said he loved her and he was very nice to her. She left with him a few days later."

Brady found he was holding his breath as his mind brought the pictures Katie's words drew to life. He heard the way her voice shook as she went on, and his heart ached for her.

"Rose came home three months later. She was pregnant, and very sick. Her empty eyes told us her life had become a rerun of Mother's. She died giving birth to a stillborn child."

Distress threaded every word. Her love for Rose was obvious in the way she said her sister's name. Finally he tied the threads together. What had happened to Rose had scarred Kate terribly.

"After Rose died, nothing made sense anymore." Kate's voice broke, before she continued, "I was on the point of dropping out of school, when Mrs. Henry called me into her classroom and told me I would be my own

worst enemy if I did that. She said I had to finish school
so I could be the person Rose wanted me to. She got me
to see the school psychologist regularly, and she person-
ally stayed on my case till I graduated.''

The dampness on her face told her she had been crying quite a while, though she hadn't noticed. Kate didn't
wipe the tears away.

"You loved Rose very much, didn't you, Katie?"

"She was my best friend."

Brady didn't know what to say or do. *Oh, Katie, I'm
the worst kind of fool there is.* His highfalutin notions
about love being all that mattered in a marriage had been
born from the nearsightedness of being part of a happy
family. He'd had no right to subject her to those little
tests he'd thought up.

He'd dismissed her poverty without finding out the
true extent of it. She had been through so much. He'd
always thought of her as a strong person, but till now, he
hadn't realized what real strength was. Kate had dragged
herself every inch of the way up in life, to get to where she
was today.

In his line of work, Brady saw men who claimed the
same past as an excuse for everything that had gone
wrong in their lives. Alone, Katie had set and achieved
some very tough goals. How could he have ever judged
anything she'd done?

She had every right to protect herself from the man
she'd thought him to be, by pretending to still see Harold. Every right to think financial security was the most
important thing in a marriage. Men made advantageous
marriages all the time. Why was it wrong for a woman to
say she wanted to?

Now he knew why Katie had mentioned over and over
the desire to give her children the best upbringing ever. It

was the only way she could get rid of some of those ugly scars the past had left on her mind.

He was grateful she'd had a friend in Arletha Henry.

"So, that's why you want to be a teacher," he said.

Hadn't Henrietta Cooper mentioned some girl Katie had helped, the very first day he'd met her?

Calmer now, she nodded. "I want to have that same power to help children. If not for Mrs. Henry, I'd be a high school dropout. I was so confused, but she made me believe in myself."

Brady started the car. To make any trite remark about her past would only add to her pain. To reach for her now in the belief that holding Katie would remove the past was ridiculous. If he held her it would be because *he* needed to be close to her. No, he had to give her time to get over sharing her story with him. For someone as private as Kate, that wouldn't be easy.

Brady had hoped she would turn to him herself. But she'd withdrawn again. The shuttered look on her face, the deep sadness in her eyes were like a Keep Off sign. He had to face the fear that had been growing all afternoon. Kate's past was bigger than anything he had tackled before. He couldn't fight it. She had been through too much to ever change, to ever take a risk on love. So where did that leave him?

"So, what did you expect?" Kate asked herself angrily. Waking at six, she sat by the window, in her rocking chair, her cold hands cupped around a mug of tea. "Did you think Brady would hear about your past and say, 'Never mind Katie. Let's get married'?"

It was a good thing he'd met Mrs. Henry. Whatever the teacher had said, had prepared him for what followed, but it still had to have been a shock to him. Brady had finally seen that their backgrounds were too disparate for them to ever be happy together. She didn't blame him. Very few men would want to marry a woman with her background.

The warm sympathy she had seen pouring out of Brady's beautiful eyes was exactly what she had dreaded. The last thing she wanted from him was pity.

If only she had done things differently. If only the past hadn't fashioned her a set of blinkers that she'd worn for too long. If only she'd been able to see money couldn't ensure happiness . . . people did. That was the only real guarantee happiness had . . . people, who, with their attitude about life and marriage, put down premiums that ensured happiness.

This past week marked the beginning of a lonely life without Brady. She could have called the five preschools that had asked her to set up an appointment for an interview, but she hadn't. Instead, she'd spent long hours at the college library making up all the classes she'd missed when she was ill. But even the usual panacea of hard work had failed to blot out thoughts of Brady.

Brady glared at the painting on his office wall. The past three days were enough to try the patience of a saint, and he'd never wanted to be one. Two of his cases coming up for trial had kept him busy night and day. Now he was free. Now he intended to court Katie the way every woman should be courted. She deserved nothing but the best.

Surely the past three days had given her time to get over the emotional storm she'd been through on Sunday. Reaching for the telephone, he dialed her number. It was time to make his next move. Now.

"Hello?"

"Katie, would you have dinner with me tonight? We need to talk."

Kate wondered why Brady sounded so stern. "Wh-what about?" she asked, her heart hammering in her chest.

"Us. We have a great deal of unfinished business to discuss."

Kate's heart sank. Being Brady, of course, he would want to tie things up neatly, write Case Closed on their file, before he got on with his life.

"Katie?"

She owed him that much. Brightly, she said, "All right, Brady. I'll have dinner with you."

"Great. I'll pick you up at six."

Brady hadn't mentioned where they were going, but Kate wanted to look her best. And knowing him, he wouldn't take her to a fast-food café. Going to her wardrobe, right after she hung up the phone, she took out a dress that had been hanging at the back. She'd bought the designer garment when she'd worked at the department store, but had never worn it.

Removing the protective plastic sheath, Kate held the dress up against her. It would give her the confidence she needed to get through the evening. She may not have had a home life she could be proud of like Brady was of his, but she'd made something of herself. She was proud of that.

There was no need for this final meeting, no need for the end to be spelled out for her, but she would go along with Brady's plan. Maybe this evening would help her get her future in perspective. No matter what, the most important thing was that Brady must never guess her heart was breaking.

Chapter Eleven

He stared at the vision in the doorway. The dress left Katie's shoulders bare, clung to her curves till her waist, and then flared out in misty shades that ranged from palest green to deepest aqua. Her hair was swept up in a new style, and her face was expertly made up. She looked like an ice princess tonight, not the warm mermaid of his dreams.

"You look beautiful."

"Thank you, Brady." Her smile didn't reach her eyes as she said, "Would you like to come in while I get my wrap and my bag?"

He nodded. Her voice was keep-your-distance formal. This wasn't going to be easy.

Kate shut her bedroom door behind her, and the sound snapped Brady back to his surroundings. He had been watching her. Looking around in an effort to regain some of his composure, Brady's gaze fell right away on the poster on the far wall. It was new.

He went close to it, his eyes narrowing. It was of a clown on a swing, but it was the clown's eyes that held him. Large eyes filled with tears, an expression mirroring a world of pain and turmoil. It tore at his heart.

Oh, Katie. Let me share your pain.

"Shall we go?"

Brady swung around. "Of course. Where did you get this?"

"A small store near the college."

Brady decided not to say anything more. To talk about the picture now would be a bad start to the perfect evening he had planned.

Kate's eyes widened as Brady got on the freeway that would take them to the beach. Was he planning dinner on the *Shenondoah?*

She relaxed slightly as they talked about Cody. Kate had taken him to the movies midweek, and then they had eaten at a fast-food place.

"He's very fond of you," Brady said quietly.

"The feeling's mutual." Cody called her every other day, and Kate had realized that easing herself out of the four-year-old's life wasn't going to be simple. Cody seemed to take it for granted she'd always be around.

When they'd exhausted the subject of Cody, Brady talked about his grandfather's home in Ireland, and the fact his parents were planning a trip back there soon.

Content to take her cue from him, Kate researched her mental files for harmless topics to discuss. As they got closer to the beach, poignant memories of her birthday returned. Kate wished Brady had chosen a different venue for their last meeting.

The picture of Brady's face, as she had blown out the candles on her cake, returned.

"I hope you'll always be happy, Katie," he'd said.

She'd thrown her shot at happiness away.

Kate closed her eyes. Tension knotted the back of her neck. She should have made an excuse not to come.

"We're here."

Kate opened her eyes, and stared. They were in a well-lit underground garage. A valet hurried to the car, and opened her door.

"Good evening, ma'am. Evening, Mr. Gallagher."

"Evening, Jacob. How's your mother doing?"

"Great, thank you, sir. My mother said to thank you for the reference you gave her. She got the job at your friend's office."

What job? Kate wondered, as Brady's hand splayed against her back. Excitement shot through her at his touch, making her stiffen, and Brady let his hand drop. A million pinpricks of disappointment replaced the earlier sensation of heat.

He led the way to an elevator and as it ascended Kate told herself they were probably going to dine at one of the rooftop restaurants by the beach.

Her eyes widened as the elevator doors swished open and she found herself looking at a living room.

"Where are we?" she asked Brady, bewildered.

"My place."

"Oh."

He took her wrap, while Kate looked around. She had watched the elevator buttons light up and knew they were at the top of the building. The penthouse apartment, done in green, gold and black looked very elegant, and yet she saw touches of Brady in the paintings of Ireland that hung on the walls.

"Katie, sit down please."

Brady cursed the uneasiness gnawing at him. He needed to be calm. Yet so much depended on... In an effort to hide the way he felt, he kept talking as he poured sparkling cider into crystal glasses and set out a dish with nuts.

Kate wondered what was wrong. Brady had never been like this before. Was he trying to tell her something? That she was just another acquaintance to be entertained with small talk? The more he talked, the quieter she became.

He'd better hurry the dinner up, thought Brady. He didn't know if he could keep looking at Katie and not reach for her. Determined not to spoil the evening by blurting his love out was proving to be hard to do.

Kate told herself this was probably as hard for Brady as it was for her. Trying to do her bit, she had just launched a discussion on the state of the environment, when he stopped talking.

The elevator swished open. Kate stopped her desperately neutral monologue in midsentence as she saw a uniformed waiter wheel in a tray covered with silver dishes. Another followed behind him.

"Dinner," announced Brady, smiling into the bottom of his glass.

Kate's gaze was riveted on the two men setting a small table by the window. The elevator doors opened again and yet another man entered. He was wearing a tux and carrying a violin case. Bowing to them, he walked over to the corner, set his case down and took out his violin.

It was all too much to take in at once. "I need to wash my hands." Kate rushed down the hallway to the bathroom door Brady had pointed out earlier.

In the elegant bathroom she stared at herself in the mirror. Was this Brady's way of pointing out the differences between them? After all, it was very hard for someone as kind as Brady was to come right out and say something like, "I don't think we really suit each other." Had he decided that showing, not telling, was a more effective way of letting her know it was all over between them?

"I'd like that table on the balcony," Brady told the waiters. As they carried it out, he hoped he'd done the right thing. He couldn't tell if Kate liked the surprise or not.

Why was she talking so much? Why was the uneasiness growing inside him? He smiled at her as she came back into the living room, taken aback by the look in her eyes. Pride nestled there with a lacing of pain.

Kate couldn't remember a thing about the dinner. She served herself the things that could be swallowed without too much difficulty, washing the food down with coffee. The music the violinist played stretched her nerves to the breaking limit. The hovering waiters seemed like birds of prey, emphasizing the fact that she could never belong in Brady's world. The backdrop of the sunset was too beautiful a setting for tragedy. Kate set her fork down, unable to pretend anymore.

It didn't take him long to figure out things were not going the way he had planned. Brady dismissed the violinist and the waiters, his gaze on the top of Katie's bent head.

As soon as they were alone, he said, "What's wrong, Katie?"

The eyes she lifted reminded him of the clown in the poster on her wall. "Take me back, Brady. I don't belong here."

"I beg your pardon?"

"I know how rich you are, Brady, how far apart our worlds are. You didn't have to arrange all this to prove it to me."

Brady felt his jaw go slack. "What on earth do you mean?"

She had nothing more to lose, so she might as well tell him. "I don't have to be hit over the head to get a fact, Brady. I know we're not social equals, but I still wish you hadn't chosen this way of showing me." She stood up and said, "Now, will you please take me back?"

He'd had enough of her convoluted mind. St. Patrick preserve him from all women! Frustrated, Brady pushed his chair back as he stood up. "It will be my pleasure."

An hour later, Brady stared at the double whiskey he had poured himself in his parents' place. Mom and Dad were spending the night in San Diego, visiting Cousin Ellen. He'd given in to the impulse to spend the night here because right now his apartment held too many memories of Katie.

The first gulp of his drink had been enough to clear away the fog of his anger. Reason insisted he think things through and pinpoint one factor before he got roaring drunk.

All he'd wanted was to treat Katie to an evening filled with romance, before he told her he loved her. He hadn't wanted to be crude and talk about money, so he'd thought he'd just show her that she'd be well provided for financially. She hadn't given him a chance.

"Women," Brady told the empty house, "were created to drive a man crazy."

Lifting his glass in a salute to the entire sex, and Katie in particular, he drained the glass.

"You look like death warmed up," Maura announced as she greeted her brother with a kiss.

"I love you, too, sis," Brady assured her as he entered the condo Friday afternoon. His head hurt, a reminder it didn't appreciate his indulgence of the night before. "Where's Cody?"

"He and Jack have gone to the Village for an ice cream." Maura went back to the list she'd been making out, waiting for the question she knew was coming.

"What's that?"

"It's a list for a small party I'm planning. I'm wondering who will suit Kate better. Sheldon St. James, the new VP in Jack's company, or Dr. Peters's nephew. You know, the one who's a neurosurgeon."

Brady stared at his sister. Did she actually have the gall to sit there and tell him she was matchmaking for *Katie?*

"I know. I'll invite them both and Kate can pick whom she likes better." Maura put her pencil down and smiled. She eyed her brother's stiff back as he stared out the kitchen window.

Brady looked out unseeingly. His anger against Katie hadn't lasted. How could it? Being mad at her was like being mad at a part of himself. The most important part. No matter what, he loved Katie. A surge of determination came over him. He wasn't going to let Maura introduce her to anyone else.

All Katie and he needed was a chance to get this latest confusion straightened out. He was done with romance...with waiting. It was time for some straight talk.

He swung around to face his sister. "Maura, I...I need your help."

His sister smiled at him. "Big brother, I thought you'd never ask."

Kate cleaned her apartment Saturday, trying to scrub the memory of Brady out of her mind. She put the glass paperweight he'd given her into a drawer. She had to forget him and get on with her life.

That useless organ, her heart, had forgotten its sole purpose was pumping blood, and had taken up aching for Brady. In addition, her brain had turned traitor, pointing out over and over again that she'd made a fine mess of everything, and she had no one but herself to blame.

Kate sat back on her heels and studied the square patch of shining kitchen floor she had been mopping. She still used a rag, instead of buying a newfangled mop, clinging to the old way of doing things, just like she had clung to her old ideas for too long.

The telephone rang, and Kate got to her feet to answer it.

"Kate? It's Maura. Listen, we're having a surprise party for my parents tomorrow, and we'd like you to come."

Kate's heart leapt. Her first thought was she would get to see Brady again. Her next was her wounds would never heal if she kept opening them up.

"I—I..."

"Please say you'll come. Jack and I want you to meet the new VP in his firm, and a single doctor we know. They're both really cute."

No. Kate was surprised at the way her mind shied away from the idea of meeting other men. The only man she wanted was Brady.

She was about to refuse the invitation, when Maura said, "Would you mind coming early and giving me a hand? Jack's going to take Mom, Dad and Cody out of the way. Did I mention we're going to have the party at my parents' place? More room. Mom's going to love it. She mentioned yesterday she wanted to see you again."

Kate hesitated. It would be rude to refuse, and she couldn't lie about having another engagement. Besides, both the senior Gallaghers had been extremely nice to her when she was watching Cody, treating her like a close member of the family, not as a mere baby-sitter.

"I'll come."

She could go there early, help Maura and then slip away soon after the party started. No one would miss her.

"We're having a barbecue, so wear something casual. See you at about three, tomorrow?"

"At three," Kate echoed, hanging up.

She bit her lip. Her head needed examining. There was no other reason for being such a glutton for punishment.

The Gallaghers' front door was open when Kate got there.

"Maura?" she called, stepping inside.

There was no answer. Setting her handbag down, Kate wondered if Brady's sister was in the backyard, arranging things for the party. There was no sign of the part-time maid who worked for Mrs. Gallagher.

Walking through the house, Kate opened the sliding doors that led from the family room to the patio. There was no one in the backyard, either.

"Maura?" Kate wondered if she'd slipped out to the store for something.

"Hi, Katie!"

"Brady." A hand at her throat, Kate stared at him. She hadn't seen him because he'd been lying on a deck chair, by the pool. She took in his black swimming trunks, his glistening skin, and backed away. "I'm looking for Maura."

"She isn't coming. I planned this, so I could talk to you. Why haven't you been answering your telephone, Katie?"

"I... I've been busy. Why didn't you leave a message?"

"Because what I've got to say has to be said face-to-face."

"No." Kate put her hands over her ears, unaware of what she was doing. "There's nothing more to say."

She didn't need Brady to spell out why they were incompatible.

"Listen to me." Brady got up, reaching for one of her hands.

"No. Leave me alone, Brady." She backed away from him, as if she didn't want him touching her.

He couldn't help it. The Irish in him took over. Before he knew what he was doing, Brady had picked her up in his arms and strode to the edge of the pool.

"Hold your breath," he said, and then jumped into the deep end of the pool with Kate in his arms.

She came up sputtering, furious, and immediately began to strike out for the side. He got there before her, and said "Katie, listen to me. I'm sorry I threw you into the pool, but it seemed the only way to cool you off. I have to talk to you and I can't do that if you won't listen."

Kate stared at him, and suddenly felt the anger drain away. She'd rather love him than hold on to her animosity.

"What is it, Brady?"

The quiver of her lower lip was his undoing. He'd meant to explain he loved her, that he had done so from the first day he'd seen her, that without her his life wasn't worth a dime. Instead he hauled her to his chest and reached for her mouth.

Kate resisted the pressure of Brady's mouth for all of two seconds. Then her lips parted and her hands gripped his head, urging him closer, so she could have her fill of him. She ran her hands up and down his back, wishing she wasn't encumbered by her wet clothes. Her hands came to rest on his hips, pausing at the waistline of his briefs. Brady raised his head and took a deep breath of air.

"I want you forever," he told Kate sternly.

"Mmm," she murmured as she trailed kisses down his chin and then went back to nibble on his lower lip.

"We're getting married as soon as possible," Brady whispered in her ear, during the next interval.

"You want to marry me?" Hands flat against his chest, Kate pushed away from him.

Drunk on her kisses, Brady threw caution to the winds. "No," he said sarcastically. "I don't really want to marry you. I want to marry the Queen of Timbuktu. I'm just getting you ready, so you can go there and tell her how much I love her."

"You love me in spite of everything?"

The glimmer of dawning wonder in her eyes made Brady feel like shouting with joy. Cradling her face in his hands, he said, "I have always loved you. I love you now, and I will always love you."

"What about my past?"

"Kate, I love you, past and all. It's made you who you are now. Warm, sensitive, caring."

He watched the tears flood Kate's eyes, and panicked. "What's wrong? Have you thought up some other reason why you can't love me?"

"I love you, but I just don't know why you would believe me, when all I did was talk of money. I thought after you found out where I'd grown up that you didn't want to have anything to do with me. I thought that you arranged that dinner just to show me what a fool I'd been—"

"Say it," interrupted Brady, running his thumb along her lower lip. They would clear up the rest later. "Let me hear you say the words again."

She placed her own hands over his and said, "I love you, Brady. I always have, but I was scared and so I fought my love for you. I love you now. I'll love you always."

Brady's mouth came down hard on hers, and Kate responded with all the passion she'd held back for so long.

"You don't know what it does to me to hear you say the words," Brady said, with Kate's head pressed against his chest. "I believe you *do* love me."

"Why?" Kate demanded.

Brady smiled. "Because I saw the love you had for me in your eyes a long time ago. I felt it in your touch, in your kisses, before you even admitted it to yourself." A hand came up and traced her lower lip again, unable to stay away, before he bent to still its trembling with the quick pressure of his mouth. "I knew we belonged together, the day you came to the store."

"You're not angry with me for lying to you about seeing Harold?"

"I lied to you, too, about being a salesman. We both had what we thought were valid reasons." Brady's finger traced the collar of Kate's pink shirt down to the second button. The first seemed to have come undone. As Kate watched, he bent and planted a kiss on her skin. "Talk about a comedy of errors. I arranged the evening at my apartment because Maura went on and on about how a little romance said more than a thousand words. I never meant to taunt you with anything."

Kate's eyes clouded. "I ruined a beautiful evening."

"There'll be many more. I would like to discuss them with you in great detail, but we better get out of here before the family returns. They said they would give me an hour—no more."

"An hour?" Kate brushed the lock of hair on Brady's forehead aside and let her fingers trail down the side of his face. She couldn't get enough of touching him.

"They said if I didn't sort my problems out in an hour, they were going to recheck the hospital records. They said Gallaghers weren't so clumsy when it came to loving, and maybe somebody had switched babies."

"We'll have to tell them about my past, Brady," she cautioned. He could joke all he liked and talk of love, but

Kate knew exactly how much his family meant to him. She didn't want to cause a rift between them.

"Tell them all you want," Brady said. "I don't care what anyone thinks, but just to reassure you, Maura and my mother think you're wonderful, regardless."

"As a baby-sitter," Kate pointed out. "Marriage is different. Everyone wants the best for their children, Brady."

"*You* are the best for me," said Brady, nibbling on her ear. "But don't worry. My parents haven't forgotten their own beginnings. My mother worked in the laundry room of a small hotel in Dublin, and my father was a traveling salesman, staying there on his first business trip. She burned one of his shirts with one of those old coal irons. Scared, she hid it, dressed up in another guest's clothes, and went to his room to beg him not to report it. Said she'd save up all her wages and send him the money for a new shirt, but if he complained, she'd lose her job."

"What happened?"

"Dad took one look at her standing there in a dress two sizes too big for her, shivering and shaking with fear, and he fell in love. He told her he didn't want her money, he wanted her to go out to dinner with him. The rest is history."

Kate lifted her face to Brady's and said, "I've made so many mistakes, Brady, but I don't want you to ever doubt that I love you."

"I won't if you remind me every day," he said, kissing her till she couldn't breathe. "Let's hurry and leave before the family gets here. Besides, I don't want you to catch cold in those wet clothes."

He pulled himself out of the pool and then reached down to give Katie a hand. The sight of their clasped hands stilled him for a moment. It was a symbol that from now on they would always be together.

"I've been working on a wedding present for you."

"You have?"

"It's an old home on five acres of land. Perfect for your project."

"Brady!" Kate wound her arms around his neck and hugged him. "You remembered what I said about the children's home."

He put a hand up and let his knuckles caress the side of her face. "I remember everything you've told me, Katie. Did you want to run the home yourself?"

Kate shook her head. "I don't have the experience, plus I still want to teach. Will you help me find a nice couple to do it?"

"I will." Brady dropped a kiss on the tip of her nose. "You know, these have been the longest seven weeks of my life. I never anticipated it would take so long to convince you we're made for each other. There were times when I thought I'd lost you for sure. Will you promise when the old memories return and make you sad, that you'll tell me about them? Our lives won't be complete unless we share every part of it, with each other, Katie— good *and* bad."

She nodded, her eyes filled with tears of joy. "No more lies."

"No more lies," repeated Brady. "Now we've got those details ironed out, there's something I have to do." From a nearby table, he picked up the rose he'd got at the florist's earlier and gave it to her. Cradling her hands in his, he said, "Katie, will you marry me?"

She looked surprised over the formality of his proposal, then laughed happily. "Yes, Brady. Yes, please."

Kate looked at him, her heart overflowing with love. How could she have ever thought that someone so right for her in every way was Mr. Wrong?

*   *   *   *   *

HE'S MORE THAN
A MAN, HE'S
ONE OF OUR

THE BIRDS AND THE BEES
by Liz Ireland

Bachelor Kyle Weston was going crazy—why else would he be daydreaming about marriage and children? At first he thought it was beautiful Mary Moore—and the attraction that still lingered twelve years after their brief love affair. Then Mary's daughter dropped a bombshell that shocked Kyle's socks off. Could it be young Maggie Moore was *his* child? Suddenly fatherhood was more than just a fantasy....

Join in the love—and the laughter—
in Liz Ireland's *THE BIRDS AND THE BEES,*
available in February.

Fall in love with our FABULOUS FATHERS!

R O M A N C E™

FF294

Take 4 bestselling love stories FREE
Plus get a FREE surprise gift!

Special Limited-time Offer

Mail to Silhouette Reader Service™

3010 Walden Avenue
P.O. Box 1867
Buffalo, N.Y. 14269-1867

YES! Please send me 4 free Silhouette Romance™ novels and my free surprise gift. Then send me 6 brand-new novels every month, which I will receive months before they appear in bookstores. Bill me at the low price of $2.24 each plus 25¢ delivery and applicable sales tax, if any.* That's the complete price and—compared to the cover prices of $2.75 each—quite a bargain! I understand that accepting the books and gift places me under no obligation ever to buy any books. I can always return a shipment and cancel at any time. Even if I never buy another book from Silhouette, the 4 free books and the surprise gift are mine to keep forever.

215 BPA ANRC

Name	(PLEASE PRINT)	
Address	Apt. No.	
City	State	Zip

This offer is limited to one order per household and not valid to present Silhouette Romance™ subscribers. *Terms and prices are subject to change without notice. Sales tax applicable in N.Y.

**Relive the romance...
Harlequin and Silhouette
are proud to present**

A program of collections of three complete novels by the most requested
authors with the most requested themes. Be sure to look for one volume each
month with three complete novels by top name authors.

In January: **WESTERN LOVING**   Susan Fox
                                          JoAnn Ross
                                          Barbara Kaye

Loving a cowboy is easy—taming him isn't!

In February: **LOVER, COME BACK!**   Diana Palmer
                                          Lisa Jackson
                                          Patricia Gardner Evans
It was over so long ago—yet now they're calling, "Lover, Come Back!"

In March: **TEMPERATURE RISING**   JoAnn Ross
                                          Tess Gerritsen
                                          Jacqueline Diamond

Falling in love—just what the doctor ordered!

Available at your favorite retail outlet.

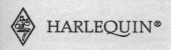

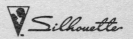

**And now for
something completely different
from Silhouette....**

SPELLBOUND
R O M A N C E

Unique and innovative stories that take you into the world of paranormal happenings. Look for our special "Spellbound" flash—and get ready for a truly exciting reading experience!

**In February, look for
One Unbelievable Man (SR #993)
by Pat Montana.**

Was he man or myth? Cass Kohlmann's mysterious traveling companion, Michael O'Shea, had her all confused. He'd suddenly appeared, claiming she was his destiny—determined to win her heart. But could levelheaded Cass learn to believe in fairy tales...before her fantasy man disappeared forever?

Don't miss the charming, sexy and utterly mysterious
Michael O'Shea in
ONE UNBELIEVABLE MAN.
Watch for him in February—only from

Silhouette
R O M A N C E™

SPRING fancy '94

They're sexy, single...
and about to get snagged!

Passion is in full bloom as love catches
the fancy of three brash bachelors. You won't
want to miss these stories by three of
Silhouette's hottest authors:

CAIT LONDON
DIXIE BROWNING
PEPPER ADAMS

Spring fever is in the air this March—
and there's no avoiding it!

Only from 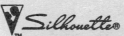 *Silhouette®*

where passion lives.

He staked his claim…

HONOR BOUND

by
New York Times
Bestselling Author

previously published under the pseudonym Erin St. Claire

As Aislinn Andrews opened her mouth to scream, a hard hand clamped over her face and she found herself face-to-face with Lucas Greywolf, a lean, lethal-looking Navajo and escaped convict who swore he wouldn't hurt her— *if* she helped him.

Look for HONOR BOUND at your favorite retail outlet this January.

Only from…

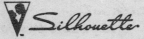

where passion lives.   SBHB

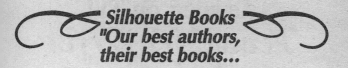

Silhouette Books
*"Our best authors,
their best books...*

DIANA PALMER
Soldier of Fortune in February

ELIZABETH LOWELL
Dark Fire in February

LINDA LAEL MILLER
Ragged Rainbow in March

JOAN HOHL
California Copper in March

LINDA HOWARD
An Independent Wife in April

HEATHER GRAHAM POZZESSERE
Double Entendre in April

*When it comes to passion,
we wrote the book.*

BOBQ1

As seen on TV!
Free Gift Offer

With a Free Gift proof-of-purchase from any Silhouette® book,
you can receive a beautiful cubic zirconia pendant.

This gorgeous marquise-shaped stone is a genuine cubic
zirconia—accented by an 18" gold tone necklace.

(Approximate retail value $19.95)

Send for yours today...
compliments of ▼ *Silhouette*®

To receive your free gift, a cubic zirconia pendant, send us one original proof-of-purchase, photocopies not accepted, from the back of any Silhouette Romance™, Silhouette Desire®, Silhouette Special Edition®, Silhouette Intimate Moments® or Silhouette Shadows™ title for January, February or March 1994 at your favorite retail outlet, together with the Free Gift Certificate, plus a check or money order for $2.50 (do not send cash) to cover postage and handling, payable to Silhouette Free Gift Offer. We will send you the specified gift. Allow 6 to 8 weeks for delivery. Offer good until March 31st, 1994 or while quantities last. Offer valid in the U.S. and Canada only.

Free Gift Certificate

Name: _____

Address: _____

City: _____ State/Province: _____ Zip/Postal Code: _____

Mail this certificate, one proof-of-purchase and a check or money order for postage and handling to: SILHOUETTE FREE GIFT OFFER 1994. In the U.S.: 3010 Walden Avenue, P.O. Box 9057, Buffalo NY 14269-9057. In Canada: P.O. Box 622, Fort Erie, Ontario L2Z 5X3

FREE GIFT OFFER   079-KBZ
ONE PROOF-OF-PURCHASE
To collect your fabulous FREE GIFT, a cubic zirconia pendant, you must include this original proof-of-purchase for each gift with the properly completed Free Gift Certificate.

079-KBZ